THE GREENES OF ROXBY HALL

Gillian Kaye

CHIVERS
THORNDIKE

This Large Print edition is published by BBC Audiobooks Ltd, Bath, England and by Thorndike Press®, Waterville, Maine, USA.

Published in 2003 in the U.K. by arrangement with the author.

Published in 2003 in the U.S. by arrangement with Jill Kelbrick.

U.K. Hardcover   ISBN 0–7540–7372–6 (Chivers Large Print)
U.K. Softcover   ISBN 0–7540–7373–4 (Camden Large Print)
U.S. Softcover   ISBN 0–7862–5726–1 (Nightingale)

The text of this Large Print edition is unabridged.
Other aspects of the book may vary from the original edition.

Set in 16 pt. New Times Roman.

Printed in Great Britain on acid-free paper.

British Library Cataloguing in Publication Data available

Library of Congress Cataloging-in-Publication Data

Kaye, Gillian.
    The Greenes of Roxby Hall / by Gillian Kaye.
        p. cm.
    ISBN 0–7862–5726–1 (lg. print : sc : alk. paper)
    1. Nannies—Fiction. 2. Nobility—Fiction.
    3. Large type books. I. Title.
    PR6061.A943G74 2003
    823'.914—dc21   2003055974

CHAPTER ONE

Mrs Fawcett, dressed in black bombazine lightened only by the silver cross hanging around her neck, glared at her daughter across the breakfast table. Laura, the youngest of the two Fawcett girls, sighed. It was four weeks since her father's death and she was sure that she had argued with her mother every day since he had been decently and formally buried in the churchyard, in the Yorkshire market town of Thirsk.

She had also argued with her sister, Jane, who had spent two frantic weeks at Spring Bank House trying to console her mother and to keep her two unruly children in order. At the same time, she attempted to persuade Laura to go and live at Petrie Lodge in Helmsley with her and her family. Lastly, Laura had argued with her kind brother-in-law. James Tempest had insisted that if Mrs Fawcett was to give up Spring Bank House to go and live with them in Helmsley, then Laura would be most welcome in his home, too.

She remembered her conversation with him now, a few weeks ago, because although she was related to him only by marriage, she liked him better than either her sister or her own mother. Laura was ashamed of these thoughts, but she put them down to the fact that she

1

resembled her dear, lost father and not her mother or her sister.

'Laura, we must speak together,' James had said, as they walked in the garden of Spring Bank House on the day after Mr Fawcett's funeral. 'While it is proper of Jane and my mother-in-law to show their grief, I do not believe that it is necessary to sit in the drawing-room all day long making their eyes red with crying and wearing out numerous lace-edged handkerchiefs.'

Laura had smiled at James's turn of phrase and his attempts at being level-headed. It was quite true that Jane and her mother had stopped crying only to eat their meals, their appetites seemingly not affected by their grief. Jane should have been giving some attention to their two children, Rob and Emily, whose energies and mischief-making activities had proved too much for their grandmother's maid. They had not brought a nurserymaid with them as the accommodation at Spring Bank House was limited.

So it was, that day in the garden, that Laura listened willingly to what James had to say. She knew what she wanted to do with her life and she also knew that it was going to be difficult to persuade her mother and her sister into agreeing with her plans.

'Laura,' James went on, 'in the first place, you must know that you are more than welcome to come and live under our roof in

Helmsley when your mother sells Spring Bank House.'

Laura spoke hastily.

'I do know that, James, and it is exceedingly kind of you when you have already agreed to have Mama to live with you, but I refuse to be a burden on you. It is not only that. You know very well that Jane and I have never agreed. It is not that I do not respect her. She is five years my senior and I think that, as a child, I was in awe of her. She always had to lord it over me and affection did not seem to enter into it. We are so different. But I know that she is a good wife to you and mother to your children and I have no wish to bring discord into a happy family. It is enough that you are giving a home to Mama. She and Jane have always dealt well together.'

She stopped speaking, wondering if she was saying too much.

'But what will you do, Laura?' James asked her. 'It was a shock to us all when you father's will was read and we discovered that his financial affairs were in disarray. However did he come to lose the fortune he had inherited from his father?'

She had no hesitation in replying.

'It was these wretched railways, though I suppose I shouldn't say that of them. I should be a forward-thinking, modern, young girl who believes that the railway is the way of carrying goods and people of the future. The canals

3

have had their day and the roads are not suitable for conveying people from place to place at any speed. You know very well how tedious a long coach journey can be. Papa was so interested in it all. Then he met Mr George Hudson of York, who is known as the Railway King, and that was the end of my sensible and thrifty father. He put money into every proposal for a new railway which he came across and there are a lot of villains out there, I am sure, trying to obtain money so that the latest railway line can be promoted. Often the surveying work was done but the proposal never got through Parliament and the money mysteriously disappeared. Poor Papa, he longed to see the day when the railway ran from York to Darlington.'

James laughed.

'It is only 1836, but I think that in only a few years' time, we will be able to get on a train at Thirsk and travel all the way to Scotland.' Laura looked at him.

'You are like Papa, James, so be warned by his disastrous dealings.'

'I cannot spare the money to speculate on the railway boom,' he replied. 'I have a wife and children to think about. But this is getting us nowhere. If you won't come to live with us in Helmsley, what will you do? There will be some money from the sale of Spring Bank House but that goes to your mother. There is no provision for you.'

4

'I shall go as a governess somewhere.'

'You? A governess?'

James sounded scandalised.

'Yes, why not? Papa gave us a good education, I am eighteen years of age and I think I would make a good governess. I am the only one who can do anything with Rob and Emily!'

The last words came as a laughing boast.

James looked at Laura closely. She was not a tall girl, but she had an abundance of lovely brown hair, a fair skin and dark brown eyes. Her features were small and delicate except for her mouth which showed a firmness, some would call it obstinacy, and character. She was, in fact, a very pretty girl and James almost said so.

'I wonder why I did not marry you, Laura,' he started to say.

She gave a chuckle.

'Probably because I was only twelve years old when you fell in love with Jane and she is a lot prettier than I am in any case. Girls with golden locks are always considered the prettiest.'

'I am not so sure,' James said, then returned to the subject of Laura's future. 'Now, what is all this nonsense about being a governess? Your mother will never agree to it.'

'No, I do not suppose she will,' Laura said. 'She will consider it beneath the dignity of a Fawcett, but as long as I know that she is safely with you and Jane, I shall be free to provide for myself in the way which I think fit.'

She looked at him carefully.

'James, may I ask you to look out for or enquire about a post as governess for me? I don't mind where I go, but if I have a choice, I think I would prefer to stay in Yorkshire. Will you do it for me, James?'

He smiled at her. He would always do as Laura wished.

'Yes, Laura, of course I will,' he replied and they then talked of other things.

Laura was remembering this conversation with James now as she faced her mother across the breakfast table.

'Mama, you know that James and Jane would have made me welcome, but their house is not large and their family is likely to increase in size.'

'Laura!'

It took little to shock Mrs Fawcett, and Laura tried not to laugh.

'Just because our family consisted of only Jane and myself does not mean that Rob and Emily are going to be the only Tempest children.'

'No, dear, of course not, dear, but I do wish you would not be quite so outspoken. As for becoming a governess, I am confident James will make you change your mind and you will come and live with us at Petrie Lodge.'

'On the other hand, Mama, James has

6

promised to look for a situation for me. Between Thirsk and Helmsley, there is sure to be a family somewhere in need of a governess.'

'It is beneath the dignity of a Fawcett, Laura.'

She has said it, Laura thought, with some glee. I knew she would say it sooner or later.

'We shall see, Mama. The important thing is to get you safely to Petrie Lodge. You can leave the running of Spring Bank House to me and I will see it safely sold and handed over. I know that you will not mind leaving the carriage and Ben—as coachman for me. James will come and fetch you in his carriage and we can have a cart to carry all your cases and boxes. No, do not start crying again, Mama. I know it is sad for you to leave the house where we have been so happy, but you must look forward. You will enjoy being with Jane so much, and I know that you will love having the children about you.'

Mrs Fawcett dabbed her eyes and sniffed.

'Yes, dear, of course, you are quite right and at least I will not have the worry I had with your father and the railways. I cannot imagine dear James ever behaving so recklessly.'

'You are quite right, Mama, for James told me so himself. Jane is very fortunate to have him for a husband.'

'I should have found someone for you, Laura, but the worries of your father's speculations and then his illness seemed to

7

consume all of my energy.'

Mrs Fawcett sounded forlorn and Laura got up from the table and walked round and kissed her cheek.

'You do not have to worry about me, Mama. I will become a governess and fall in love with the eldest son and will end up being a countess or a lady something in no time at all.'

Laura hoped to cheer her mother up but did not succeed.

'A governess is a very poorly-paid post, Laura. You must know that.'

'I shall do well, Mama. Do not worry about me and go off to your dear ones in Helmsley.'

This was achieved with great effort and persuasion two weeks later. James came to fetch his mother-in-law in their carriage, together with a small cart to take the luggage. Laura was pleased to see him but he did not have good news for her.

'Laura, my dear,' he said when they were on their own for a moment, 'I have to report total failure in finding a family in need of a governess. In fact, the nearest I have been able to achieve is the post of nurserymaid with Sir Henry and Lady Greene who live at Roxby Hall near Ellerton. It is not all that far from here. I believe the village to be somewhere between Northallerton and Thirsk.'

Laura was immediately interested.

'But I know of them. Papa knew Sir Henry in the old days, I believe. I remember that his

8

first wife died and he re-married and has a young family. Papa lost touch with him when Sir Henry married again and then, of course, he could think of nothing but his railways. What do you think about it, James?'

He looked at her very seriously.

'A governess is one thing, Laura, a nurserymaid would be quite unsuitable for a Fawcett.'

Laura laughed but did not mean to sound ungracious towards him.

'You sound just like Mama, James, and I shall want you on my side. I think I will send a letter to Sir Henry Greene and we will see if he thinks I am suited to the post. By the time I receive a reply, you will have returned to Helmsley and Mama will be safely settled in with you at Petrie Lodge.'

It was James's turn to laugh.

'I do not think it is the slightest use arguing the point with you, Laura. I will let you give my name for a character reference.'

She reached up and kissed him.

'You are the best of brothers,' she told him.

Things happened quickly after that. Spring Bank House was sold very easily, and Laura also sold the carriage. Then sadly, she had to ask Ben to find another position. For herself, she bought a dog-cart and kept her faithful mare, Whisky, to take her about Thirsk or as far as Helmsley if she wanted to visit the family.

9

Then a reply came from Sir Henry Greene and Laura thought it encouraging. She read it through several times.

My dear Miss Fawcett,

Thank you for your letter. I was saddened to hear of the death of your father and Lady Dorothy and I send our sincerest sympathies. I am also saddened to know that you have been left in such unfortunate circumstances. I would not normally consider a young lady of your birth and upbringing as an applicant for a post as nurserymaid, but my wife and I would like to see you to discuss it.

The fact is that our daughter from my first marriage is the same age as yourself and I do believe that we might be able to combine a position of companion to Janice with that of caring for the younger children. I imagine that you must still have some form of transport and if you would like to come and stay at Roxby Hall for a few days, we can discuss the matter and you will be able to become acquainted with Janice and the children.

Yours sincerely,
Sir Henry Greene.

For almost the first time, Laura found herself wishing that she was not on her own. True she had the good Mrs Snainton as her

10

housekeeper but she could hardly discuss such matters with her, or could she?

She is a sensible woman, Laura said to herself, and she has known me all my life. Why cannot I ask her opinion?

She found Mrs Snainton in her little sitting-room near the kitchen and told her of the contents of the letter she had received. To her alarm, Mrs Snainton burst into tears.

'Oh, Miss Laura, to be sure it ain't right for a young lady like yourself to go into service, for that's all it is when all's said and done. Your poor father will not rest easy in his grave, that he won't.'

But Laura was made of sterner stuff.

'If it wasn't for my poor father dabbling in investments in the railways, I would not be in this position, Mrs Snainton.'

The housekeeper wiped her tears.

'It is true, and you are quite right, Miss Laura. I must be sensible for we've got to do the best for you. I am all fixed up now that I'm getting older and can go and live with my sister in Carlton Miniott, but we've got to find a home for you seeing as how you refuse to go and live with Miss Jane and the children and that dear Mr Tempest, to say nothing about your mama. But here I am, going on when what I really want to say to you after your kindly showing me the letter is that you couldn't wish for a better family than Sir Henry Greene of Roxby Hall. My sister's

11

youngest has been cook there ever since the first Lady Greene were alive, and a dear lady she were, too. It were very sad her going like that, but they do say as the new Lady Dorothy Greene is a very fine lady and as how lucky Sir Henry is to find such a nice lady and them with the little children when the older ones are grown up and I do believe as Mr Aubrey manages the estate for his father.'

'So you think I should go and see Sir Henry?' she said.

'If you're that set on it, Miss Laura, you couldn't do better and it looks as though you might make a friend of Miss Janice Greene into the bargain.'

'Mrs Snainton, you are a dear and I will write to Sir Henry straight away and try and go over there next week. We have a month before we hand over the house.'

So it was that on the first day of June, Laura found herself in her dogcart, her hands on Whisky's reins, driving quietly along the streets of Thirsk and out along the country lane that would lead to the village of Ellerton which lay several miles from Thirsk. She did not know the district well as it had been the family's custom to favour Helmsley and the moors which lay beyond the small Yorkshire town. Then Jane had married James Tempest of Helmsley and any visiting was always in their direction.

Ellerton was a tiny village but it boasted a

church, an inn, a blacksmith's and a small shop which appeared to sell everything, served as the letter receiving office and had the local bakery attached to it. Laura made enquires at the shop and was told, yes, Roxby Hall was just through the village, two or three miles farther on but not as far as Breckenbrough. This interested Laura as she knew that her father had been acquainted with the owner of Breckenbrough Hall.

Roxby Hall, she found when she reached it, was not an old house but was imposing. It had been built in the local stone at the end of the last century and had columns round its central porch. Laura was not sure whether to drive round to the stables or to leave Whisky with the dog-cart in the gravel circle in front of the house. She decided on the latter knowing that Whisky would wait patiently.

As she got down from the cart and started walking towards the house, the front door opened and a young lady, very much Laura's age, came down the steps and then halted as she reached the bottom step. She was dressed in a simple dress of dark red, with the fashionable fitted bodice reaching into a point at the waist, the skirt was full and undecorated.

Laura, in contrast, had put on over her dress a fitted coat of dark green velvet which was worn with a plain hat which did not hide her curls entirely. The two of them stared at each other, and this was not surprising as they bore an astonishing resemblance to one another. They were the same height, both with pale complexions and dark eyes. The young lady, pausing on the bottom step, spoke first.

'Who are you?'

Laura, wondering if this was the daughter Sir Henry had spoken of, took a step forward and smiled.

'I am Laura Fawcett. I have come to see Sir Henry Greene.'

'Goodness gracious, you cannot be the new nurserymaid who is also to be a companion to me. You are a lady.'

'Yes, I am afraid I am. Do you think Sir Henry will turn me down?' Laura said and tried not to sound anxious.

The young lady was smiling now.

'It is most extraordinary. Do you think we are alike? I do believe we could pass for sisters.'

Laura was still smiling.

'I was just thinking the same. Are you . . .'

She hardly knew how to form the question.

'Yes, I am Janice Greene and I have been looking after my young stepbrother and sisters, but now that I am eighteen, Papa thought it right to have a proper nurserymaid. You don't look in the least bit like a maid of any kind.'

'Oh, dear,' Laura said, but she gave a short laugh. 'And I put on my plainest coat and hat, too.'

'Come along in and I will go and find Papa.'

Laura followed Miss Janice Greene up the steps and as they entered the front door, they met a gentleman on his way out. He was very tall, formally dressed and scowling.

'Aubrey,' Janice exclaimed, 'look who I've found. She is going to be the new nurserymaid.'

Laura met dark eyes and an even darker scowl.

'She doesn't look in the least like a nurserymaid to me,' he snapped and ran down the steps and out of view.

CHAPTER TWO

Inside Roxby Hall, Laura stood with Janice in the large, imposing entrance hall.

'That was my brother, Aubrey,' Janice said. 'I am sorry for the surliness. He is pre-occupied with this business of the railway.'

Laura looked puzzled.

'How does it affect you out here?' she asked.

'They have started to plan the line to Northallerton and are threatening us with surveyors and engineers and all sorts of unwelcome proposals,' Janice replied. 'But let us forget unpleasant things. I must take you to my father. I expect he is in the library.'

Laura followed Janice through the hall which was laid with colourful rugs and hung with rather sombre-looking landscapes in oils. Janice flung open the door of the library and Laura heard her voice.

'Papa, here is Miss Laura Fawcett to see you and I must tell you that . . .'

She was not allowed to finish.

'Not now, Janice. I must see Miss Fawcett first.'

Janice turned to Laura, smiling.

'Let him see for himself,' she whispered.

So Laura went into the room and stood by Janice's side. Sir Henry Greene stood up to

16

greet her. He was a man of medium height, with grey hair and a pleasant expression. Then he stepped round his desk and walked towards them, holding out his hand to Laura, chuckling at the same time.

'Miss Fawcett, I am pleased to meet you, and I see now what Janice was going to say to me. There is an extraordinary likeness between the two of you. I do believe you could be taken for sisters. Now leave me with Miss Fawcett, Janice. I will call you if I wish to speak to you, but I am pleased that the two of you have met.'

He turned to Laura.

'Do sit down, Miss Fawcett. I am pleased that you have come even if you are not in the usual run of nurserymaids. I will tell you a little of the family. Aubrey is my eldest son and manages the estate for me, and Janice you have just met. She is eighteen and we have a very suitable marriage arranged for her. Since my first wife died—she was Janice's mother, of course—Janice has been very good in helping Lady Dorothy with our younger children, Samuel, Fanny and Jessica, all of them under seven years of age and not yet old enough for a governess. I feel I must have the right person for them as children of that age are easily influenced. Now I will ring for my wife and you can tell us about yourself.'

Seconds later, the door opened, and a young woman of no more than thirty years

17

entered the room. Laura thought that she was poised and handsome rather than pretty and she was smiling very pleasantly.

'Lady Dorothy, my wife, Miss Fawcett. Dorothy, dear, this is Miss Laura Fawcett who has come to enquire about the post of nurserymaid to the children.'

Laura was not surprised to hear Lady Dorothy's first words.

'But you are just like Janice in looks. How singular. Has Sir Henry told you about Janice?'

Sir Henry spoke quickly.

'No, I have said nothing as yet. I thought it best to wait until we were both here, Dorothy.'

He looked at Laura.

'Miss Fawcett, you find yourself in uncomfortable circumstances. Please tell us something of yourself, and why you think you would make a good nurserymaid. It is most unusual for a lady to play the nurserymaid.'

Laura was finding both Sir Henry and his wife very pleasing. She would be open with them.

'I will be honest with you and tell you that it was a shock to the whole family when we discovered the extent of my father's foolish investments in the railways. I believe they are calling it Railway Mania and that is just what it is. There are too many promoters seeking too much money and fortunes are being lost. I am sorry, I shouldn't let my views be known, but it has all brought ruin to our family. Mama has gone to live with my sister and I must find employment.'

'Or a rich husband,' Sir Henry said with a smile.

She smiled back.

'That is not so easy, Sir Henry. But it seems to be that it is not easy to find a post of governess either. Perhaps I am too young. That is why I was prompted to write to you.'

'You did not wish to go with your mama?'

Laura shook her head.

'I must be truthful. My sister, Jane, does not live in a big house and she and I have never seen eye to eye. She is a lot older than I am and I think she considers me forward and modern. So I thought it over and decided, without success, I am forced to say, to try for a post as governess.'

'You have experience with young children, Miss Fawcett?'

'Oh, yes,' Laura replied. 'I have often looked after my niece and nephew if Jane has been unwell. They are both of them under five years of age.'

'Good, good,' Sir Henry said thoughtfully and looked at his wife who smiled back and gave a nod. 'Miss Fawcett, I believe I have told you that Janice has been looking after her sisters and young brother. They love her. I do not want to take them away from her altogether at the moment. But we must tell

19

you that we have arranged a marriage for Janice with Sir Rowland Hutton of Holly Grange near Thornton-le-Moor. It is not far from here and he is a wealthy man and keen to have our daughter as his wife.'

'Janice is pleased with the match?'

Laura hardly knew why she had said it for it sounded critical, but the feeling had been conveyed that it was a marriage not to Janice's taste.

'I will be truthful, Miss Fawcett. Janice is not grateful for our efforts. She imagines herself to be in love with the young curate at Ellerton and I regret to say that we do not consider him to be a suitable husband. He is an admirable young man but he is not in a position to support a wife and family.'

He paused.

'If you come to live with us, I know that Janice will be pleased to have a confidante and friend, and that is why we are both inclined to the suggestion that you and Janice care for the children together and that you act as a companion for Janice. I have to tell you that both Dorothy and I regarded it as a stroke of good fortune when we received your letter. You would, of course, be paid a companion's salary and not that of a nurserymaid. Now I am not going to ask you to make up your mind straight away. Walk in the gardens with Janice and let her take you to meet the children. After that you can come back and tell us of

20

your decision. Would that suit you?'

Laura's head was in a whirl at what seemed to be her good fortune though she felt sympathetic towards Janice.

'Thank you, Sir Henry, Lady Dorothy. You have been very kind and most generous and I am sure I would be glad to accept.'

She found Janice waiting for her by the front door and was greeted cheerfully.

'I am sure that Papa approved of you, Miss Fawcett . . . no, I am going to ask if I may call you Laura for I feel certain that we will become friends. Shall we walk in the gardens? The children are out there somewhere with Patsy, one of the maids. She likes taking them out.'

'Didn't she want to be the nurserymald?' Laura asked.

'I think shc would have liked it but she was considered too young. She is not much more than twelve years old so I am afraid she is condemned to a life of lighting fires and scrubbing floors. She doesn't seem to mind though. She is the eldest of a large family in one of our cottages and I think she feels it a privilege to work here at the big house.'

They stopped at the top of the steps which led down to the formal part of the garden. Laura noticed that Whisky and the dog-cart must have been taken to the stables.

'I did not know that this part of Yorkshire was so lovely,' she remarked. 'We seem to be

21

higher up here and you can see for miles. What is that village? And there seems to be a big house nearby.'

'The house is Breckenbrough Hall and the village is Kirby Wiske. Beyond that is Thornton-le-Moor where Sir Rowland Hutton lives. Have you been told about him?'

Laura was not surprised that Janice had seized the first opportunity to talk about her proposed marriage.

'You are going to marry Sir Rowland, Janice?'

'No, I am not.'

The words were like an explosion.

'Janice!'

'Oh, Laura, I am so pleased to have someone to talk to and I hope you will decide to stay.'

'Janice, I must tell you that I believe that your mother and father would like me to come so that I can persuade you that the marriage would be a good thing for you. They did not say so exactly, but I took their encouragement to mean that. I think you had better tell me about Sir Rowland and the curate.'

'Come and sit on this seat. You can look at the view and listen to me at the same time.'

Laura was not at all sure that she was doing the right thing and yet at the same time, she had the feeling that Sir Henry had expected it. He had even referred to her as being Janice's confidante.

'Tell me about the curate,' she said.

'He is not to be referred to as the curate. He is the Reverend Hugh Rutherford and he is in charge of the parish at Ellerton. It is his first church and he has been there for nearly two years. He hopes to get preferment to a bigger parish soon with a proper vicarage. Then we will be able to be married.'

Laura was surprised that Janice had spoken quietly and sensibly. She had expected another outburst.

'But, Janice, you cannot . . .'

But Laura was interrupted by a cry from Janice.

'Oh, Laura, here is Patsy with the children and Hugh is with them. He has probably come to see Papa about the railway. It is all they talk about these days. Papa does like Hugh, you know. He just considers that he is not in a position to support a wife and family. I suppose Papa is right but I am willing to wait. I don't mind how many years it is as long as I don't have to marry Sir Rowland. I will have to tell you about him later. You will come to Roxby Hall, won't you, Laura? I think you have been sent by the gods.'

By this time, Laura was wondering what kind of person the object of Janice's affections was going to be. She watched with interest as the small group approached. Then it was all fun and laughter and introductions. The three children, introduced as Samuel, Fanny and

Jessica, threw themselves at Janice's full skirts. She hugged them all to her. Her face was full of delight, then Laura saw her look shyly up at the young clergyman who was standing there watching them.

Laura was intrigued. She had somehow expected a young Adonis, but in front of her was a young man of average height, slim build, sandy hair and side whiskers, and very blue eyes. If it had not been for the merriment and affection in his expression, he would have passed only as being very ordinary. Janice was speaking shyly.

'Laura, this is the Reverend Hugh Rutherford, curate of Ellerton.'

She turned to the young clergyman and smiled.

'Hugh, this is Miss Laura Fawcett. She has come to see Father about the post of nurserymaid, but dear Papa thinks that if she will accept, she could also be a companion for me. What do you think of that?'

Laura received a handshake and a smile from the young man.

'Miss Fawcett, I am very pleased to meet you. You are astonishingly like Janice in looks, did you know? I trust you are as sweet-natured as she is.'

Laura was pleased with him. He spoke with confidence and good humour, and she could tell by the way he looked at Janice that he adored her.

'I am very pleased to meet you, sir,' she started to say.

'No, please, call me Hugh as Janice does and I will call you Laura. It will be good news for us if you are to move into Roxby Hall. Janice and I have started a campaign against the worthy and rich Sir Rowland. It is proper of Sir Henry and Lady Dorothy to seek only the best for Janice, but you will realise that in my calling, wealth is not regarded as a prime virtue. It will be interesting to learn of your opinion when you have met Sir Rowland.'

He turned from Laura to Janice.

'Janice, my dear, I will leave you with Laura and the children. I must speak to your father on a matter of some urgency.'

'Yes, Hugh, of course. I will see you after the service on Sunday.'

Janice smiled after him and then spoke quietly to Patsy.

'You take the children indoors, Patsy. I expect they will be glad of a drink after their walk. It was good of you to take them for me this morning.'

'It were a pleasure, ma'am,' Patsy replied and the three children ran up to the house with her.

'What do you think of him?' Janice gasped.

Laura was both amused and astonished. The Reverend Hugh Rutherford seemed to her to be a very modest and proper young gentleman and not one to make a lady's heart beat faster, but it was evident that he and Janice were genuinely attached to one another.

She felt that she could understand Sir Henry's objection to him as a suitor for his daughter in material terms, but it seemed to her that Janice was young and it would not hurt her to wait a year or two until the Reverend Hugh had a respectable living. But she must ask Janice about Sir Rowland.

'The reverend seems to be a very amiable gentleman, Janice, and very attached to you, but tell me what it is you have against Sir Rowland Hutton. I am sure that your father would not force you into an alliance for which you have a distaste.'

Janice gave a long sigh.

'I am so glad you have come, Laura. You will stay, won't you?'

Laura smiled.

'I think I am destined to somehow, just as you said. Now, about Sir Rowland. I feel I must know the whole story.'

Janice spoke soberly.

'He is actually a friend of my step-mama's family. You know that my own mama died, Laura? But I am very fond of my step-mama. She is Lady Greene really, but we call her Lady Dorothy so that she won't be confused with my mama. She is much younger than Papa but they are very happy and I am glad for him. I am telling you this because Sir Rowland is nearer to my step-mama in age. He is nearly forty. That is over twice my age and he seems very old.'

'But why should your father choose someone so much older than you? I don't think I understand.' Laura sounded puzzled.

'To tell you the truth, I think he was worried that I would run off with Hugh. We do love each other, you see, but Hugh would never behave like that. He is very respectable and proper and I admire him for it.'

'So your father thought that if he arranged an advantageous match for you it would make you forget about Hugh?'

Laura was beginning to understand.

'Yes, it was done with every good intention, and Sir Rowland is very keen on the match. He has never married. I think he has enjoyed the good life too much.'

This last was said with some bitterness and Laura glanced at the pretty girl who was so much like herself in looks if not in character.

'You do not like him, Janice?'

'I loathe him. Oh, it is not just because I love Hugh so much. If there was no one else, I would still loathe Sir Rowland Hutton. Oh, Laura, I can tell you things I cannot even mention to Hugh, it is so disgraceful. Sir Rowland is a good-looking man, I do not deny that. He is also rich and has a beautiful house but that does not weigh with me. But he takes liberties with me, Laura. I do not know how to tell you and yet it is a relief to me to be able to talk to someone.'

Laura stopped her.

'Do not tell me anything you might regret afterwards, Janice.'

'No. You must know the truth if you are coming to live here. You might even have some influence with my father.'

'I doubt it,' Laura said wryly. 'Don't forget that I am coming here as the nursery maid. Not only that but I do think that your father expects me to persuade you away from the Reverend Hugh.'

'Never,' Janice declared with some stubbornness. 'I will tell you the whole truth and you will understand. Papa and Mama always leave me on my own with Sir Rowland, to become better acquainted with him, I suppose, but as soon as they disappear, all Sir Rowland wants to do is to kiss me, and fondle me, not in a very nice way. Hugh has never kissed me. He would not dream of anything so improper when we are not engaged. But Sir Rowland is quite the opposite. He puts his arms round my waist in a most personal way and pulls me up against him so that I cannot get away without making a dreadful fuss and a struggle. I have been able to tell no one and I don't know how I can bear it any more. You see, he is so circumspect when Papa is there and they think he is the perfect gentleman.'

She stopped, lost in thought for a moment.

'Laura, I am only eighteen and I do not know a lot about life but I am certain that the way Sir Rowland treats me is not proper. He just laughs at me when I protest and says he loves me, yet I am sure he doesn't. Then one afternoon last week—oh, I don't know how I can tell you. I was in a morning dress which had little buttons up to the neck, and he held me very tightly and undid the buttons and pulled my dress right off my shoulder. I was never more ashamed, but I managed to break away and run out of the room. He was roaring with laughter at me and saying what fun he was going to have when we were married. Laura, tell me truthfully, do you think I am just young and innocent? Should I have enjoyed all that behaviour? I am sure it was wrong.'

Laura had left Janice to run on for it seemed important for the girl to unburden herself. She was the same age as Janice but she felt a lot older, perhaps because of having an older sister and a devoted brother-in-law. She was shocked at Laura's confession but she knew that there was a certain type of gentleman who would behave in such a fashion. She would have to choose her words carefully for it was quite obvious that Sir Rowland Hutton would not do for Miss Janice Greene. Laura was reluctant to make revelations to her prospective employer before she had settled down in the house and knew the family better.

'Janice, I am shocked by what you have told me and I will do all I can to help you, but you must give me time, my dear. Just think, Janice, if I am going to live here then I can stay by your side and you will have no need to see Sir Rowland on his own. Perhaps it will all improve from now on. Would you like to leave it to me to handle Sir Rowland for you? I could even start a little flirtation with him!'

Janice's eyes stared at Laura in amazement.

'You are a complete hand, Laura. I do believe you could steal Sir Rowland from me, but I would not wish to have you endure such indignities.'

'Janice, you are a dear, sweet girl and you deserve your nice Hugh. I will do all in my power to secure him for you. Now, come along, I must go and tell your father that I have decided that I would like to come to Roxby Hall.'

It took very little time to speak with Sir Henry again and it was agreed that Laura would take up her duties at Roxby Hall at the end of the month. She was shown her bedroom which was large enough to be used as a sitting-room as well, and she was told that she could keep Whisky and the dog-cart as Sir Henry thought that it would be useful for taking the children out on little trips. She left the library feeling that she was being treated more as one of the family than as a servant.

Janice saw her off and she walked round to the stables. Turning the corner of the house, she almost collided with the tall gentleman who had been introduced as Janice's brother, Aubrey. He put out a hand and took her arm to steady her and they found themselves staring at each other. Laura had a strange feeling of hostility mixed with attraction which she could not explain.

'Is it true that you are to be the new nurserymaid?' he asked abruptly.

'Yes, sir.' Laura thought it was the correct way to address him. 'I have met your sister and I have spoken to Sir Henry and he has kindly agreed for me to come as nurserymaid to the children and as companion to Janice. We are to look after the children together.'

'Are you indeed? I understand you are a Fawcett. Are you from Spring Bank House or Petrie Lodge? I think I know your sister and her husband.'

'I must tell you that Spring Bank House has been sold and I have been forced to find employment. I consider myself very fortunate in finding a place here at Roxby Hall.'

'A rum do, if you ask me. You don't sound like a nurserymaid, don't look like a nurserymaid. Perhaps you could charm Sir Rowland Hutton away from Janice. I don't like the idea of her being married to a man of his reputation and I have told my father so. She would be better off with her curate.'

Laura felt an annoyance at his tone.

'I have met the Reverend Hugh Rutherford and consider him to be a very pleasant young gentleman.'

'So he is, so he is, no harm in him and he is against the railways just as we are. But it will be years before he will be in a position to marry and Father seems to want Janice settled. Can't understand the rush, myself.'

He stopped and looked at her piercingly.

'Shouldn't be talking to the nurserymaid like this. Damned awkward the position you are putting yourself in. Good-day.'

And he was gone. Laura walked over to Whisky and the dog-cart.

I don't think I am going to like Mr Aubrey Greene, she was thinking, though I do not suppose I will often have occasion to meet him.

CHAPTER THREE

By the end of June, when the newcomers were due to arrive at Spring Bank House, Mrs Snainton had settled in with her sister at Carlton Miniott, and Laura found herself packing an old leather trunk of her father's and preparing herself for her removal to Roxby Hall.

She was so busy, she had no time to grieve over her departure from the only home she had ever known, though it was a sad day when she had to say goodbye to Mrs Snainton who shed more than a few tears.

She settled down very quickly at Roxby Hall though she found that there were one or two problems of etiquette to be resolved. The most immediate was that of meal times and provoked an argument amongst the family. They were all in the drawing-room discussing the matter and Laura found that Sir Henry was unsure of what to do, which seemed unusual for him. Janice was pleading with her father.

'Couldn't Laura have her meals with us in the dining-room, Papa? She is like a friend to me already. You cannot expect her to eat in the kitchen with the servants.'

'She is a servant, Janice,' Aubrey said. 'If she is paid for her services then she is a servant.'

'You are horrid, Aubrey,' his sister said. 'Not everything has to be according to the rule book.'

'My dear sister, I think you should know that there is a strict protocol amongst the servants. Cook eats in the kitchen at the head of the table, Mrs Bainbridge as housekeeper has her meals in her sitting-room.'

Laura thought she should interrupt the argument.

'Perhaps I should have my meals in my room, Sir Henry.'

Aubrey spoke quietly in return.

'That would be rather lonely for you, Laura.'

It was the first time he had called her by her name and her glance flew to his face. She detected a kindly look in his eyes, unusual, as he was usually most formal.

'I don't mind being on my own,' she replied.

'How about having your meals in the nursery with the children?' he suggested cheerfully. 'You might be able to teach them some table manners.'

Everyone laughed, but Laura said she thought it was a good idea and even Janice could not disagree.

A little while after that, Laura met Aubrey as he was coming down the stairs. He seemed a little more approachable than he had been.

'Thank you for coming to my rescue, sir,'

she said gladly.

He looked at her.

'I will not have you calling me "sir",' he objected.

'But you insisted that I was a servant and you were quite correct.'

'That was a point of etiquette and did not echo my sentiments,' he said brusquely.

What a strange man he is, she thought.

'Whatever do you mean?' she asked him.

'You have got yourself into this ridiculous position and it is difficult to know how to behave towards you. You take a post as a nurserymaid, you become the finest friend Janice ever had, and you are a lady. I would like you to call me Aubrey, but it would not do. Mr Greene is too formal though correct but sir is impossible.'

'Shall I call you Mr Aubrey?' she suggested.

'That is what Mrs Bainbridge calls me as though I was one of the children. Would you like to call me Mr Aubrey?'

She nodded.

'Yes, I think I would. It sounds just right. Why do you seem so distracted?'

As soon as the question was out, Laura regretted it, but it was true that sometimes she found him human and approachable, but more often he was distant and snappish.

'Am I distracted?' he replied, then gave a disarming grin. 'Yes, I suppose I am. It is all because of this business of the railway.'

Laura frowned.

'I thought I was the only one affected by the railways. My father lost a fortune in investments in hopeless schemes, yet I do believe the railway to be a good thing.'

He glared at her as he had done before.

'You do, do you? And what do you see good in travelling by rail instead of by carriage, I would like to know?'

'I would have thought it was obvious,' she stated and thought to herself, that she sounded quite rude, and must do a little better.

'Just think of getting from Yorkshire to London for instance. It is several days' journey by carriage with stops at coaching inns on the way. Once there is a direct link between York and London, it will take only a day to get there on the railway.'

'So Miss Fawcett would like to travel,' he said scornfully.

'I am not saying that I would need to go to London myself, but there are many people who do business in the capital. It would be very convenient, and think of letters, too. They could be delivered on the same day as being posted.'

'You are obviously in a hurry.'

Laura started to feel angry.

'There is no need to laugh at me and mock me. I see the railway as the means of travel of the future. Just think of Thirsk as it is at the moment. It is a busy market town with strings of pack horses going through and with wagons and mail coaches as well as the private carriages, gigs and phaetons. All the goods could be sent on the railway and it would make the roads clearer for private traffic.'

'And what if the railway runs through your back garden, Laura?'

She stared.

'You are talking nonsense.'

'Nonsense, is it? Well, listen to this, young lady. We have heard rumours that the line up to Northallerton is to be extended and the proposal is to lay the track straight through the grounds of Roxby Hall.'

'Oh, but they cannot do that.'

The words were out before she could stop them.

'Aha, you are changing your tune. Just come out to the front porch with me and I will show you.'

He opened the door for her and Laura stood at the top of the steps with him, looking at the view she admired so much.

'Now look, Laura. Down through the formal garden and across the park, do you see a large wood?'

She nodded. She had noticed it before, promising herself to walk as far one day.

'Yes, it is a lovely wood.'

'It is not only a lovely wood, it is a very ancient one. There are trees in the wood which are hundreds of years old, and there is an oak, a very special one, which we believe to be nearly five hundred years old. And now we are told that they want to take the railway through the wood, which has always been called Fox Wood. We do not know for certain yet for the engineers and surveyors for the railway company have not approached us. I can tell you, Miss Laura Fawcett, that they will take a railway through that wood over my dead body.'

Laura looked at him. He was looking over his landscape with pride and passion. She suddenly saw him as very handsome. Then he continued as though he had not broken off.

'You will find that I am very fierce on this subject, but I will be honest with you. I am not against the railways as such. I agree with you about their speed and efficiency, but there is no need to go tearing up acres of beautiful parkland just to keep the track in a straight line. I am sorry, Laura, I am afraid that I get very heated on the subject. I think you will find that Janice's Hugh is of the same mind. Some of his Ellerton cottagers are likely to lose their homes.'

'Are you expecting a surveyor or engineer?' she asked him.

'Any day now we are expecting a deputation from the railway company. So if I were you, I would keep out of my way. I do not vouch for my temper.'

This was said with such good humour that she smiled up at him.

'I think I will have my hands full with the children and protecting Janice from Sir Rowland, Mr Aubrey.'

'Good girl,' he said and laid his hand on her shoulder in farewell. 'I think I am glad that you came to us.'

She watched him run down the steps and round to the stables. He was dressed for riding and she guessed that he was going round the estate. She could feel the firm touch of his fingers through her dress and found that she liked it.

No more was said of engineers and surveyors for the railway after that and the problem was removed from Laura's mind by a visit from Sir Rowland Hutton. Laura had no idea that he was expected, in fact afterwards she thought he had come over without warning in order to inspect the new female at Roxby Hall. She was going downstairs to the drawing-room, expecting to find Janice there. They had not decided what to do with the children that day.

She found the drawing-room empty of anyone of the family, but by the window, looking out over the park, was a tall gentleman, dressed in style. His top hat and cane were both held in one hand so that when he turned to greet her, he held out the other hand with seeming pleasure.

'My dear Janice ...'

He broke off and Laura almost laughed

39

aloud at the surprise on his handsome though rather plump features. In fact, he gave the impression of a suave inclination to the portly which she did not like at all.

'Well, I declare you are Janice's double and I must assume that you are the new nurserymaid who is also a companion to Janice. Miss Laura Fawcett, I believe, and I must introduce myself for there is no one here to perform the honour. I am Sir Rowland Hutton and it is my hope to marry dear Janice in a short while.'

He had taken her hand in his and was holding it closely in a warm and intimate clasp which she did not like.

'And may I call you Laura, Miss Fawcett? It gives me great pleasure to meet you.'

Laura had withdrawn her hand and was watching him as he talked. Her first instinct was one of revulsion, at the intimate clasp of the hand, the admiring eyes, the gushing tone. She had the impression that those eyes were searching under the lace of the chemisette which she was wearing, for modesty's sake, in the low neck of her summer dress.

He will not do for Janice, she was thinking. I understand everything now, and I can imagine that his behaviour in front of Sir Henry and Lady Dorothy is faultless. The germ of an idea came to her and she wondered if she might not be able to detach Janice from Sir Rowland. Perhaps she could even promote the curate in

Sir Henry's eyes.

I'll try, she told herself.

'Sir Rowland, it is indeed a pleasure to meet you. I am becoming very fond of Janice and I do feel that I would like to know you better.'

'Can't detach her from that damned curate, can you?'

'Oh, Sir Rowland, Janice does love the young man but it is a hopeless case as far as her father is concerned. And why should she look to a penniless curate when she has such a fine gentleman as yourself offering for her hand?'

Laura could not believe that she was capable of such insincerity, but her words had the desired effect. She saw him raise his hand to his dark moustache and touch it as though he was preening himself.

'Why, Miss Fawcett, no, I will call you Laura, for I think we are going to deal extremely well, I do believe that your coming to Roxby Hall is going to have an uplifting effect on us all. You have more spirit than little Janice whom I find a trifle insipid, dear girl though she is. I think I will make up my mind to visit more often, and of course, you and Janice will come and visit me at Holly Grange. It is less than an hour's drive away.'

'I am afraid that my first duty is with the children, Sir Rowland.'

'Bring them, bring them all, and Janice can look to them while I show you round the

Grange. She has seen it before, but I am afraid its splendour does not impress her. You will be far more appreciative, I feel sure.'

'It will be a pleasure, Sir Rowland.'

'Do call me Rowland, my dear, for I can see that we are going to be the best of friends.'

'I know my place, Sir Rowland. I am the nurserymaid.'

Laura was wondering how long she could keep up this charade and was glad when the door opened and Lady Dorothy and Janice appeared. Enough is enough, Laura thought, I have made a good start.

'Sir Rowland,' Lady Dorothy cried. 'And have you met Miss Fawcett? It is so nice for Janice to have a young lady of her own age in the house. I cannot think of Laura as the nurserymaid, you know, for she is one of the Fawcetts of Thirsk. Now, Janice, I am sure you would like to take a turn round the garden with Sir Rowland.'

Janice was an obedient girl but the expression on her face told Laura instantly that to be on her own with Sir Rowland was the last thing she wanted. Laura spoke directly to Lady Dorothy.

'It is such a lovely, warm morning, Lady Dorothy, that Janice and I thought we would take the children to the shrubbery. They love a game of hide-and-seek.'

She turned and looked Sir Rowland full in the face.

'Sir Rowland, do let us all go together. I would very much appreciate the chance of getting to know you better. I have heard such glowing reports of you from Janice.'

'But, Laura,' Lady Dorothy began, slightly put out.

She was swiftly interrupted by Sir Rowland.

'No, do not object, dear lady, it would give me the greatest of pleasure.'

'We will go and get the children,' Laura said. 'I don't think they will need coats today.'

She took the arm of a stunned Janice and they hurried from the room. Janice could not speak quickly enough.

'Laura, whatever are you about? I have never heard such . . .'

Laura took her arm.

'I have it all in hand. Do as I say and follow my lead. I have thought of a way of dispensing with the splendid but repugnant Sir Rowland. Don't ask questions, Janice, for I am not sure of myself yet. I will find a way, that is all I can tell you.'

'Very well, Laura,' Janice said quite meekly.

If Samuel, Fanny and Jessica were impressed by their visitor's splendid appearance, they did not show it. They had met Sir Rowland before and they gave him a polite greeting, then raced off to the shrubbery which lay at the side of the house. There was a stone seat in the shade at one end and Laura made sure that Janice and Sir Rowland sat down together. She ignored the pleading look in Janice's eyes and went off to play with the children.

In her very full skirts, it was difficult for her to hide behind any bush and she was easily found by the children and their squeals of delight and laughter filled the air. Then, pretending exhaustion, Laura sank down on the seat at Sir Rowland's side and exhorted Janice to go and join the game.

'It is your turn, Janice. I will sit and keep Sir Rowland company and perhaps we will get to know each other a little better.'

Janice went off thankfully and in a daze of incomprehension. What kind of game was Laura playing?

Laura was sitting close to Sir Rowland and she smiled up at him.

'Is it not delightful out here, Sir Rowland?' she began. 'Does Holly Grange have a large garden like this?'

'Yes, indeed, Laura. I even have a maze and I must tell you that I should not object to getting lost in it with you.'

Laura gave a false trill of laughter.

'Oh, la, Sir Rowland, we would never get lost because you would know the way out, but I would like to try it with you, and do you think the children could come? They would love a maze and you could rescue them if they got hopelessly lost.'

He put his hand on her arm and she could feel the pressure of his fingers through the thin

44

cotton of her dress. She almost shivered with dislike and forced herself to stay calm and pleasant.

'Laura, I hope you will visit very soon. It has been a pleasure to meet you this morning and I must tell you that you have captured my admiration and if it had not been for my arrangement with Sir Henry . . . no, no, I must not think such wicked thoughts. I am promised to dear Janice. Ah, here she is now. Janice, I must tell you that I like your new nurserymaid very much. In fact she is the most unlikely nurserymaid I have ever met, but I can see that she is very good with the children. Now both of you young ladies can take my arm and we will walk back to the house. I feel quite honoured.'

As they reached the house, Aubrey rode up and jumped from his horse to greet them. He took in the scene and his eyes met Laura's. There was a sparkling question in his expression but she refused to return it and spoke to Sir Rowland.

'I hope it will not be too long before we meet again, Sir Rowland. I must take the children up to the nursery now.'

'Goodbye, Laura. I will just have a quiet word with Janice and then I must go and find Sir Henry. I want to ask him if he is bothered with this railway business which seems to threaten us.'

Laura nodded, refused to look at Aubrey and took the children into the house. She left them in the nursery and went to fetch them some drinks. She came out of the door and found her way blocked by Mr Aubrey Greene. He grasped her by both arms and pulled her towards him.

'What are you doing, you Jezebel? You are making eyes at Sir Rowland. I could see what was going on and he loved it. Don't tell me you are trying to steal him from Janice. Only a baronet's daughter will do for Sir Rowland, you know. Are you playing some deep game?'

She laughed up at him.

'I am, but this was only the first move and I am not telling you any more.'

'Laura, you don't really want Sir Rowland for yourself, do you? Though I suppose he would certainly be the answer to your financial problems.'

'Mr Aubrey, I will tell you quite honestly that I loathe Sir Rowland as much as Janice does, and I cannot bear to see the poor girl married to him. My next move is to have a talk with the Reverend Hugh Rutherford. Then we are going to make a visit to Holly Grange and I am going to get lost in the maze with Sir Rowland.'

'You really do mean to try for Janice's sake, don't you? But don't play with fire, young Laura. You are far too nice a person to get burned by the likes of Sir Rowland Hutton.'

He tightened his hold.

'You will always come to me if you are in

trouble, won't you?'

'Yes, Mr Aubrey, I will, and now I must get the children their drinks. They are hot and thirsty after all that running about. I think you had better go and lend your chaperonage to your sister.'

'Yes, miss. Certainly, Miss Laura.'

He grinned at her and ran down the stairs.

The next day was not so fine and rain threatened from the west. Laura looked at the dark skies and made a sudden decision which meant involving Janice in a subterfuge. Breakfast was over and they were all in the nursery, Samuel with his nose flattened to the window pane.

'I don't think we can play hide-and-seek today,' he said. 'I could hear it raining in the night and it sounded very heavy. I think it is a jigsaw day.'

Laura was pleased with this remark for it suited her scheme nicely.

'You are right, Samuel, and I think there is more rain on the way from the look of the sky.'

She turned to Janice who was sitting with Fanny and Jessica, reading them a story.

'Janice, would you mind if I took the dog-cart into Ellerton? I have written to my sister and I would like to take the letter to the letter-receiving office. It is handy having one in Ellerton.'

Janice smiled as she replied, 'Yes, of course, Laura. We can do a jigsaw together. Which one would you like to do, Samuel?'

'The one with all the zoo animals,' he replied without hesitation.

And so it was that on a damp morning in July and with a Paisley shawl over her shoulders in case of rain, Laura was to be found with Whisky's reins in her hands on the short journey into Ellerton. Laura had indeed written to Jane and her mother, so her first visit in Ellerton was to the letter-receiving office in the village shop. But the main purpose of her visit, and the one she had kept secret from Janice, was to seek out the Reverend Hugh Rutherford.

She was directed to his cottage but the little maid who answered the door dutifully said that no, the reverend was not at home. She thought he was down at the church. As it was mid-week, Laura could not imagine that Hugh was conducting a service and she made her way to the small church, leaving the dog-cart at the gate.

Inside, the church was dim as the small windows were all of stained glass and on that dull day, no sunshine shone through them to send beams of light on to the wooden pews. At first, Laura thought the church was empty and felt disappointed, but as she walked forward, there was a movement in the choir stalls near the altar.

She stopped still and then saw the young clergyman she sought walk towards her. He called her name.

'Laura, whatever brings you here?'

Then a note of anxiety came into his voice. 'Is Janice not well?'

CHAPTER FOUR

Laura stood still and let Hugh reach her. He looked very young and indeed was no more than twenty-four years. At Oxford, he had read for the church and this was his first preferment. He was wearing a grey cloak slung over his dark suit and he held his head high.

On reaching Laura, he shook her hand.

'I trust it is not bad news, Laura.'

'No, Hugh, of course not. It is a miserable day and Janice is doing a jigsaw with the children. I had to come into Ellerton on business and thought I would seek you out. Your little maid said that I would find you here. I hope I have not interrupted your devotions.'

Hugh laughed and took her by the hand, then sat with her in one of the pews.

'You have interrupted my weekly writing of the Sunday sermon. I always do it here because there are so many callers at home, either that or visits to be made. Please don't think that I am grumbling, but a clergyman has to have peace and quiet if he is to write a good Sunday sermon, you know! You wish to speak to me, Laura. I can tell by your face. Is it something serious?'

What a nice young man, Laura was thinking. It is no wonder that Janice loves him.

'You love Janice, Hugh?' she asked him.

He looked surprised at her question but made a straightforward reply.

'Yes, I love her very much but my case is hopeless. I cannot hope to get a better living for several years and how can I ask her to wait that long? She is under such pressure to marry Sir Rowland Hutton. I know it is a splendid match for her, Laura, but she dislikes him so much. I do believe the poor girl would elope with me if I would allow it, but it would wreck all our lives. I keep trying to think of a solution and I pray for one, too, but it always comes back to doing my duty to Janice and to the church. What can I do, Laura?'

Laura had made up her mind to help Janice and it only needed Hugh to show that he was honourable to steady her resolve.

'Is your financial situation really impossible, Hugh? I am sorry if it seems impertinent of me to ask.'

'I don't mind what you ask me, Laura, for I know you are a good friend to Janice. It is quite impossible. I just keep myself in food and coal and candles. How can I support a wife and maybe a family? I do not blame Sir Henry and Lady Dorothy wanting to do better for their daughter. I am sure I will feel the same one day. But if only it had not been Sir Rowland Hutton I could have borne it. I will put it bluntly, Laura. If he did marry Janice, I do not think he would be faithful to her.'

Laura was inclined to agree but did not say so.

'Hugh, I have a plan to try and get her out of the marriage. It came to me yesterday and I made my first move. My second task was to come and make sure that you really loved Janice. No, don't ask me what it is I am trying to do for I am telling no one. I would just like to be able to help the two of you. The one thing I will tell you is that I dislike Sir Rowland as much as Janice does.'

Hugh looked at her with a smile which was full of curiosity.

'Laura, you are the oddest nurserymaid I have ever met. The nurserymaids of my childhood were all young and wore blue uniforms!'

Laura laughed then.

'I have been very lucky at Roxby Hall, and Janice and I have become good friends.'

'It is Janice who is lucky,' he told her, helping her to her feet. 'I will not ask you questions but let you plan your wicked deeds on your own. I have to come over to see Sir Henry tomorrow.'

'The railways again?'

'Yes, they are threatening to pull down some cottages here in Ellerton. They are not quite on Sir Henry's land, but it is a concern to us all.'

'The march of progress?' she asked him.

'It is progress at a price if you should ask me

52

my opinion. The railway companies seem to think that they can draw a straight line from one town to another and disregard everything that might lie in between. I am afraid it is quite a hobby-horse with me.'

'It is with Aubrey, too.'

'You like Aubrey?'

'I am not sure. We are inclined to disagree, but I believe that he is not in favour of the match with Sir Rowland Hutton. That is to his credit.'

They walked out of the church and he helped her up into the dog-cart.

'I am sorry I stopped your sermon writing,' she said as she waved goodbye.

'It was a pleasure, Laura.'

Back at Roxby Hall, the days slipped by with continuing rumours of the railway being surveyed and constant visits from Sir Rowland. The trip to Holly Grange was planned and Sir Henry insisted on sending Laura, Janice and the children in the carriage.

It was a very hot day in July when they made the journey and in the carriage the children complained of the stuffiness and the heat. Sir Rowland received them graciously. He was very proud of the old house which had been in his family for generations. Laura could understand his desire to continue the name of Hutton in that place. Janice was not so defensive with him as she usually was and this seemed to put him in a good mood. Laura thought it was because Janice felt the safety of having her with her.

They were given a light meal on their arrival and once it was finished, the children could not wait to explore the maze. They walked over the lawns to reach the maze which had been made from sturdy beech hedges over one hundred years before. Sir Rowland had the ordering of the pairs to start off along broad paths and high hedges.

'Samuel, I trust you to take Fanny, and Jessica can go with Janice. I will follow with Laura and go straight to the centre. If you get really lost, you are to stay where you are and call out loud and I will come and rescue you. Don't forget you must aim to get to the centre then find your way out again.'

Janice was looking at Laura with a mischievous grin which seemed to say, 'Sir Rowland has taken a fancy to you. I am free for once,' and Laura was pleased that Janice did not object to losing Sir Rowland's company.

It is the other way round today, she said to herself and I must make the most of the opportunity. There followed nearly an hour of shrieks of laughter from the children and a promising conversation between Laura and Sir Rowland. He offered her his arm and led her through the beech hedges straight to the grassy circle at the centre of the maze where they sat together on a wooden seat. No one could see them and Sir Rowland lost no time in his pleasantries to Laura.

'I think I organised that very well, don't you, Laura? You know that you intrigue me.'

'Oh, Sir Rowland,' she said in return. 'There was I thinking that I would get lost in the maze with you and what fun it would be, and now you have brought me straight to the seat at the centre. You have spoiled it all!'

'My dear Laura, we can still have some fun together.'

Laura moved away from him and pretended coyness.

'Oh, whatever do you mean, sir?'

'Come and sit close to me, my dear. You are lovely in your golden stripes and your waist is so slim.'

Laura had put on a morning dress of gold striped satin which she thought was rather gaudy for a country visit, but she had chosen it to appeal to Sir Rowland and she had been right.

'Let me put my two hands round your tiny waist,' he said close to her ear. 'Do let me try.'

'Sir Rowland, that is not the way to behave. I do believe you are flirting with me. Oh, Sir Rowland.'

She gave a pretence of a shocked laughter as his hands encircled her waist.

'Just a quick kiss, Laura, before the others find the centre.'

He did not wait for a reply but pulled her

towards him and planted a kiss on her lips. Laura pulled away immediately, but smiled up at him coquettishly.

'Sir Rowland, I do declare I am not safe with you, and you are promised to Janice. No, not another kiss, sir. I can hear Jessica's voice and that can only mean that they are very near.'

'You tempt me, you wicked girl,' he started to say but had to break off as Janice brought an excited Jessica, who was only four years old, into the centre of the maze.

The little girl ran up to Laura.

'We found you, Laura! We didn't get lost. But I don't know where Samuel and Fanny are.'

Sir Rowland stood up.

'Don't worry, I will look for them. I can hear their voices quite near.'

He was gone and Janice looked at Laura suspiciously.

'Laura, I do believe you are flirting with Sir Rowland! You are up to some mischief, I can tell. But I don't want to upset Papa, you know.'

Laura put a hand out to Janice, saying, 'It is all going splendidly, Janice. Stop worrying.'

'He kissed you,' Janice said accusingly. 'You should not let him take liberties with you, Laura.'

'My dear Janice, although we are the same age, I have seen more of the world than you have. I was always used to having James and his friends in the house when they came to visit Jane.'

Janice nodded.

'You are quite right. I have had a very sheltered life and Hugh was the first young man ever to take notice of me. I was too young to interest Aubrey's friends, you know. But I do trust you, Laura. Ah, here they come. I will give them a drink. Sir Rowland's cook kindly made some lemonade for them. I have the bottle and some cups in the basket.'

The children chattered happily, and Sir Rowland made sure that he stood close to Laura as Janice poured out the drinks. Then Samuel, Fanny and Jessica ran ahead to find the way out with Sir Rowland helping them when they went wrong.

The pleasant summer days that followed were rudely interrupted by the first signs of activity from the railway company.

Hugh had ridden over to tell Aubrey and Sir Henry that the surveyor had been seen in Ellerton and that the deputation had already visited their neighbouring landowner whose estate extended as far as the town of Thirsk. It seemed, Hugh explained, that a single surveyor was sent on ahead to make a report on the lie of the land.

Laura had been getting to know Aubrey a little better and she grew to like him. Sometimes he would treat her with reserve and suspicion as though her dual rôle did not please him. At other times, he would join Janice and herself if they were out with the children and on these occasions, he pretended to play the big brother and these were happy moments.

Laura remembered afterwards that their troubles started on the first day of August. It had been decided at the outset that Laura would have one day off a week but no free evenings. Laura considered this generous. She did not always take the free day, but would sometimes fit the children into the dog-cart and take them down the lanes or sometimes, she would go over to Helmsley to visit Jane and James.

Summer was passing, but August was still hot. That morning of the first of August, with Janice getting the children ready to play in the garden, Laura was standing on the steps of the porch, wondering what to do with her day. She was feeling energetic and in the distance, she could see the wood which Aubrey had pointed out to her as being threatened by the railway. Even as she was thinking of him, Aubrey came out of the front door and stood at her side. He had a brooding, dark look about him.

'Whatever is it, Mr Aubrey?' she asked him.

'What usually puts me out of temper, Miss Laura?'

He had taken to calling her Miss Laura and it was as a private joke between them.

'The railway?'

58

'Yes, the damned railway and I do not apologise for my language in front of you.'

His tone was belligerent.

'Has Hugh been over again?' she asked gently.

'Yes. He came last evening. The surveyor has been snooping round Ellerton again and Hugh is worried about those cottages. He doesn't know exactly where the track is planned, but he is almost certain that they plan to demolish the cottages. It seems that a railway track can only run in straight lines. It had better not run through Fox Wood, that is all I can say.'

And he said no more but stalked off to the stables for his horse. Laura watched him go with some amusement.

I shall always remember Mr Aubrey Greene just like that, walking to the stables in high dudgeon, she thought. Then she paused in her thoughts as it struck her that she was not going to spend the rest of her life as a nurserymaid at Roxby Hall. There would come a day when she would no longer know Mr Aubrey and the notion made her inexplicably sad.

She watched him ride off in the direction of Ellerton and guessed that he was going to visit Hugh.

I must take myself for a good, long walk, she muttered to herself, and I know where it must be, just in case Sir Henry and Mr Aubrey lose their battles with the railway company and Fox

Wood is no more. It was a sobering thought. She went quickly upstairs and changed into the half-boots she kept for longer walks, then popped into the nursery to tell Janice where she was going.

'It is too far, Laura,' Janice said immediately.

But she set off through the length of the gardens and across the fields and parkland where the cattle were grazing. The land at Roxby Hall sloped very gently down to the River Swale and on the other side of Fox Wood, it was flat and uninteresting.

Laura was thinking of the railway as she stepped out. Her dress was full but did not impede her progress and she could see the beauty of the wood as she approached it. Although it was August and the leaves on the trees had lost their fresh green, she appreciated immediately the mixed, deciduous nature of the wood.

She found a path through it quite easily and walked more slowly, glad of the shade and the coolness under the trees. She saw that there were beeches, elms and oaks very close together, but there was no mistaking the old oak of which Aubrey had once spoken. The wood had been well-managed and the magnificent tree stood in an open glade at the centre of the other trees. Successive owners had given it room to spread and Laura could see immediately how Sir Henry and Aubrey felt about the desecration of the wood by the railway company.

I have to agree with them, she was thinking, but her thoughts were disturbed by a movement. She stood still and absolutely quiet and she saw emerging from behind the tree a man in a knee-length coat of rough tweed, close-fitting breeches and boots. He was wearing a hat and he puzzled her. He did not look like a gentleman but neither was he a countryman.

He was looking around him, then up at the oak. He paused, took out a notebook from his pocket and wrote something in it. That done, he walked on and Laura realised that she was right in his path. He glanced up as he seemed to realise that someone was standing there. He stopped and took off his hat, revealing a head of rough hair.

'Well, well,' he said and his tone had a familiarity which was tinged with the insolent. 'Fancy Dick Hopgrove finding a beautiful young lady in the wood. Seems my luck is in today. First the oak and now the . . .'

Laura cut him short. She had not moved and he was now confronting her.

'Who are you and what are you doing here?' she asked. 'Are you from the railway company?'

'The railway company?' he mocked her nastily. 'Of course I'm from the railways, sent to have a look for the big oak we've heard so much of. Looks as though it's got to come down, don't it, miss?'

Laura did not lose her nerve.

'It will not come down. None of this will come down. You won't even get access to the wood to survey it properly, let alone lay any track.'

'So we won't, eh? Well, you're a nice little piece. Say you and me strike a bargain. You come in them trees with me and I'll report the wood's not suitable for a track to be laid.'

She stared at him, unable to believe the coarse suggestion, knowing that she was on her own and unable to defend herself against a man of his size and strength.

'You would not dare lay a hand on me,' she said boldly though she did not feel in the least bold or brave.

'Wouldn't I, miss? Well, you've mistaken Dick Hopgrove then.'

And before she realised his intent, he had seized her in his arms. Her scream echoed through the glade and with all her strength, she tried to pull herself away. At the same time, she heard a thunder of hooves and in seconds, rough hands had pulled her away from the intruder who received a punishing blow to the head and fell to the ground. Then all she knew was that she was in Aubrey's arms. She heard her name on his lips and she turned and was gathered against him.

'Miss Laura, was I in time? Did he harm you?'

Laura was still in a daze.

'No, he did not hurt me, but how did you know I was here? And, Mr Aubrey, I think you have killed him.'

'Knocked out, that's all. Was he from the railway company?'

'Yes. I saw him write a note in a little book when he saw the oak tree. I confronted him.'

'Oh, Laura, you should have turned and run away. What did he have to say for himself?'

Memory came back to Laura and she buried her face against his chest.

'What is it, little one?'

She had never heard him speak in such a soft tone and without lifting her head, she told him what had passed between her and the stranger.

'I'll kill him,' he swore.

But neither of them had noticed that while they were in each other's arms, the man from the railway had come round, quickly risen to his feet and was slinking off through the trees.

Laura did not know that Aubrey was carrying a gun until she heard the loud report.

'Aubrey,' she cried out.

'I've missed him,' he said ruefully, for they could hear the sound of running footsteps and then the galloping of a horse as the railwayman made a hasty retreat. 'But that's what they'll get if they come again. And it won't be a pistol either. I'll bring my heaviest shotgun.'

'Mr Aubrey, you mustn't talk like that. If any of them gets killed, you'll end up in prison for manslaughter.'

He laughed harshly, then saw her worried face and his tone softened.

'Would it worry you if I was put in prison, Miss Laura?'

She looked up at him. What a strange mixture he was, uttering harsh deeds and soft words almost in the same breath.

'Of course I would care and think of your poor father and mother,' she replied carefully.

'I think Father would have done the same.'

He looked around him.

'Did you have time to look at the wood? Have you seen the oak?'

'Yes, and it is noble and beautiful. It can't possibly be chopped down for a railway.'

He gave a chuckle.

'I am glad you are beginning to see our way of thinking, Miss Laura. I think we are going to have trouble though. We have heard that the deputation is coming to see Father tomorrow.'

'I thought it would be soon, that is why I came to the wood today before the trouble starts, but, Mr Aubrey, how is it that you were here just at that very moment? It cannot have been a coincidence.'

'No, my dear, it was not. I went to see Hugh after I had left you and when I got back, Janice told me that you had gone to the wood. I knew from what Hugh had told me that there were surveyors snooping about, presumably to report back to the deputation from the railway company. So I rode as fast as I could and arrived in the nick of time.'

'It was like a miracle,' she confessed. 'I have never been so frightened in all my life.'

They were standing in the shade of the oak and he looked down at her.

'I liked holding you in my arms, Miss Laura,' he said.

'I quite liked it, too, Mr Aubrey,' she replied with a smile and felt shy yet forward at the same time.

'We must do it more often,' he said and put his hands on her shoulders. 'Look at me.'

She looked up and met smiling, dark eyes.

'I will have to take care of you,' he said. 'Now let me give you a kiss. It will be a brotherly one and we will go back and tell poor Janice that you are safe. She was worried about you.'

He bent to touch her lips with his and the brief kiss lingered as each of them found it difficult to break away.

'Thank you, Miss Laura,' he said and Laura felt the beating of her heart. 'Now we must be practical. I will take you up before me on my horse and we will be home in no time at all. I should think you could manage astride in that full dress or is it more ladylike to ride side saddle?'

They both laughed and the tension between them eased. Laura liked the feeling of his arm about her as they rode back to Roxby Hall.

CHAPTER FIVE

Before that day was over, Hugh had ridden hastily over from Ellerton, wanting to see either Sir Henry or Aubrey on what he considered an urgent matter.

Everyone was pleased to see the young clergyman, but Laura could see that something was worrying him. She also noticed Janice's face go pink with pleasure as he was shown into the drawing-room. The children were safely in bed and Laura was free.

Sir Henry, sensing that Hugh had come on business and not in pursuit of his eldest daughter, took Aubrey and Hugh into the library. The news from Hugh was that their neighbour, Mr Francis Gregson, had seen the deputation that day and had been told that the plan for the Thirsk-Northallerton railway would entail the destruction of three cottages on the edge of Ellerton. The whole village was owned by Mr Gregson and he was a good landlord, having care for his villagers and the state of their cottages.

Mr Gregson had asked Hugh to ride over with the latest news for Sir Henry and to say that Mr Gregson would drive over himself after the deputation had been to Roxby Hall, and that they could discuss the crisis together. When their consultation had finished, Hugh went back into the drawing-room looking for Janice. The two of them walked in the shrubbery together.

'Are you still bothered by Sir Rowland?' Hugh asked her.

Janice smiled.

'It has been a lot easier since Laura came,' she told him. 'It is not just that there are always two of us when he visits, but Sir Rowland seems captivated with her. I have accused her of flirting with him but she just laughs at me. I am sure she has something up her sleeve, but she won't tell me what it is. I do believe she is up to no good in the nicest possible way.'

'She came over to Ellerton to see me. Did she tell you?'

Janice looked at him, puzzled.

'She didn't. What did she want? She is not flirting with you too, is she?'

Hugh laughed.

'No, of course not. I had the feeling that she was trying to find out if I really loved you.'

'Oh, Hugh, what did you tell her?'

Janice knew very well what his answer would be but she was never tired of hearing it.

'I told her the truth and I also told her that I would not marry you while I was still a curate. I may have to wait years before a better living comes my way, Janice.'

'I would wait for you, Hugh.'

He took her hand and lifted it to his lips.

'Bless you, my dear. I do know that, but it is no use saying it to your father as long as he is set on Sir Rowland Hutton. And I suppose Sir Rowland is going to enter into this business of the railway, too. It seems the line will run very close the Thornton-le-Moor. So we shall be seeing even more of him, curse him.'

Janice looked shocked.

'Hugh, a clergyman does not speak like that.'

'This clergyman does when faced with the likes of Sir Rowland. Perhaps we could marry him off to Laura.'

'Hugh!' Janice said, scandalised. 'Laura is my friend and I would not wish him on to her. In any case, I have hopes of Aubrey and Laura.'

'Do you indeed? Do you suppose that Aubrey would marry the nurserymaid?'

Janice's laugh was merry, her heart lighter when she was with Hugh.

'You know very well that she is no ordinary nurserymaid. Poor Laura, I feel very sorry for her.'

'And she feels sorry for you. What a pair you are. But I am glad that she is keeping Sir Rowland out of your way. I am always afraid that I will knock him to the ground if he is here when I ride over.'

'I will make sure that the two of you are kept apart,' Janice said.

She was holding his hand in both of hers.

'I will wriggle out of the marriage somehow, Hugh, and I will wait for you for ever and ever.'

'That does not sound in the least practical, my dear one. We will wait until the business of the railway has been resolved. May I kiss you, Janice?'

'It is not proper when we are not engaged,' she said primly knowing that she would welcome a kiss from the man she loved in place of having to endure the embraces of Sir Rowland.

'I think we might be allowed a touch on the cheek.'

He grinned and bent and did just that, a soft brush of his lips on her cheek and she coloured with the pleasure of it.

'Thank you, Hugh,' she whispered.

The deputation from the railway company arrived in two carriages in the middle of the following morning. It was headed by Mr William Fortescue who introduced himself as chief engineer and surveyor for the company. Those with him, seated around the library, were either surveyors or accountants.

Sir Henry sat with Aubrey. They both looked very solemn having agreed between them not to let any of the company set foot in Fox Wood.

Mr Fortescue spoke at length of the achievements already made by the Great North of England Railway, building the line from York to Darlington. The next stage was to be the one from Thirsk to Northallerton, passing through Kirby Wiske and Otterington. He went to great lengths to assure them that the necessary investment had been raised, and that if their surveyors could complete their task by November that year, he would hope to have Royal Assent by the following year. The works could go ahead and he hoped that the line would be opened, together with the necessary railway stations, some four years later.

It was at this point that Sir Henry stopped him. He spoke gravely.

'Mr Fortescue, how can you hope to complete a survey by that statutory date if you encounter obstacles and opposition from the landowners along the route of the proposed line?'

'Sir Henry,' Mr Fortescue replied smoothly, 'it has been our good fortune between York and Thirsk to encounter very few difficulties. The planned route was very flat to begin with and this, of course, meant few cuttings and no tunnels to be constructed. And I must inform you that we have had only one objection for this section of the route and that is from your neighbour, Mr Gregson. I hope that we will have similar good fortune when we start to do the survey across the land of Roxby Hall. You are not opposed to the railways, are you?'

Sir Henry looked at Aubrey and nodded.

Aubrey stood up.

'Mr Fortescue, my father and I favour the progress of the railways and look forward to the day when perhaps it will be possible to travel from Thirsk to London, but this progress is at a price. If the line were to be built along our flat meadows at the side of the River Swale, then we would have no objection, but I understand from one of your surveyors that the route is planned through the wood on our property which is called Fox Wood.'

'And how did you acquire this information, might I ask?' Mr Fortescue said, still very smooth.

'From one of your men. I do not see him here today. He was found in the wood making notes about a valuable oak tree we have there.'

'From my information, sir, you attacked the man and knocked him to the ground and when he ran off, you fired at him. Is that your response to a respectable surveyor of the railway company?' Mr Fortescue asked coldly.

Aubrey was motionless, but could feel the anger creeping up inside him as he thought of Laura.

'You are unfortunate, Mr Fortescue, in your choice of words. The man in question was far from respectable. My father's nurserymaid was walking in the wood at the time and was accosted by him. He made a most improper suggestion to her and was struggling to overcome her when I arrived on the scene. I

72

knocked him down and when she had told me what he had said to her, he ran off and I fired at him. Unfortunately I missed him.'

'You are making a serious allegation, Mr Greene. I know nothing of all this,' was the stiff reply.

Aubrey's temper got the better of him and he said what he had made up his mind he would never reveal.

'You know nothing because it was too disgraceful to repeat. He said in so many words to her, that if she would go into the bushes with him, he would report to you that the wood was not suitable for the laying of a railway.'

'Aubrey!' his father exploded.

In the room, there was mayhem. All the surveyors were talking at once, names were bandied about and Mr Fortescue had sat down and was consulting the man who seemed to be his chief surveyor. Aubrey stood still, breathing heavily.

Forgive me, Miss Laura, he said to himself as Mr Fortescue stood up again.

'Might I ask, Mr Greene, if you know the surveyor's name.'

'I believe it to be Dick Hopgrove.'

Again there was a buzz in the room. Mr Fortescue frowned.

'Mr Greene—Sir Henry—you must accept my apologies and believe that I thought that I had a team of trustworthy men. Hopgrove will be dismissed instantly. I hope that this incident does not mean that you will deal in like manner with my surveyors in the future. They will have to survey the wood, as you will realise.'

Sir Henry stood up immediately. He turned to Aubrey.

'Sit down, Aubrey, you have played your part,' he said. 'Mr Fortescue, this is the first I have heard of the regrettable incident, and I will give full support to my son in his treatment of your surveyor. I will also tell you, here and now, that if any of your men strays into the wood, he will be dealt with in a similar manner, however good a character you might give.'

He paused and then continued with great force and meaning.

'Fox Wood will never be touched to make way for a railway line. It is an ancient wood and that oak tree alone has been there for five hundred years. As I said, I would give permission for a track to be laid in the lower meadows even though we would suffer from the noise and smoke from the steam engines, but through Fox Wood, never.'

'You are meaning that you would oppose my men?' he was asked.

'I would oppose them and with force if necessary.'

'I think you are mistaken, Sir Henry. It is not a vast area that is involved and I think you will discover that it will be surveyed without you knowing anything about it.'

'And I think you wrong, Mr Fortescue. I will ask you and your surveyors to leave at once. I do not expect, or have any wish to meet you again.'

The deputation crept out and Sir Henry sat down heavily in his chair.

'Aubrey,' he muttered, 'it was not really Laura who was involved?'

'Yes, it was, Father. Janice told me she had gone to the wood and I was alarmed. Hugh had just told me there were surveyors about. I got there just in time and I am sorry, but I knocked the man down and then fired at him.'

'You did right, my boy. And Laura is all right now?'

'Yes. She is made of stern stuff, your nurserymaid.'

'You will not repeat what you have said to anyone, will you, Aubrey?' his father asked him.

'No, of course not. I simply wanted to ruffle them and show them that they are not welcome here. I think we had better put our heads together to decide how to defend the wood, andd perhaps Francis Gregson had better come in on it as well. With all the men on his estate together with our own, we should be able to deter a bunch of surveyors.'

Little else was talked of for the next few days and Sir Henry drew up a schedule of his gamekeepers, farmers and farm workers to guard the wood. The same was done in Ellerton for Mr Gregson's cottages and Hugh had the ordering of that.

Then Sir Rowland arrived on the scene. The deputation had reached Thornton-le-Moor, having encountered no obstacle in between Roxby Hall and the land owned by Sir Rowland Hutton. The big house at Breckenbrough was well distant from the proposed line and from there it would run through low fields with only the narrow road from Kirby Wiske to negotiate.

Sir Rowland had an interview with Sir Henry and afterwards went in search of Janice. He found the drawing-room empty and went back to the library to ask where the ladies were. He was told by Sir Henry that Lady Dorothy and Janice had taken the children in the carriage into Thirsk to visit a cousin of his wife's. He had no idea where Miss Laura was. He imagined that she might be in the nursery taking the opportunity to tidy the room and the play things while her charges were absent.

Sir Rowland knew where the nursery was as he had often visited Janice there in the days before Miss Laura had come to Roxby Hall. The thought of being on his own in the nursery with Laura made Sir Rowland bound up the stairs with a hopeful step. Laura, indeed, was doing some sorting through of the old toys while the children were away. When there came a knock on the door, she somehow thought it must be one of the maids bringing her a cup of chocolate in the middle of the morning.

'Come in,' she called gaily in answer to the knock, then glancing up and seeing that it was Sir Rowland, she hesitated. 'Oh, it is you, Sir Rowland.'

'Laura, how delightful to find you on your own for once.'

His tone was both smug and insinuating.

Be careful, Laura, she said to herself. Here is your chance but you must take it very slowly.

She stood up and held out her hand to him very formally. He took it in both of his.

'I am afraid that Janice is not here,' she said. 'She has gone to visit cousins in Thirsk with her mother and the children. You can see that I am making the most of their absence by having a turn-out of the toys.'

She looked up and gave what she hoped was an encouraging smile.

'Would you like to help me until their return? They will be here soon.'

Sir Rowland, dressed as usual in the height of fashion, sat on a chair beside her.

'Delighted, fair lady. Now tell me, what you would like me to do?'

Laura thought she was going to enjoy the following scene.

'There are two jigsaws here which are all muddled up in their boxes. If I give you what I think are the right pieces, will you fit them together and find out if any pieces are missing? We will sit at the table together.'

'My dear Laura, I have not done a jigsaw since I was a little boy and I remember the only jigsaw we had was one of all the counties of England to be fitted together. It was not an easy task but I am sure it was very educational. These look much more interesting. You seem to be giving me all pieces of cats and dogs.'

'And I have got the picture of King Arthur and his knights. I am sure we cannot mistake the pieces. I must tell you that it is much more fun sorting out the jigsaws now that you are here, Sir Rowland.'

His put his hand on her bare arm and she did not move. He moved it in a caress and Laura had to hold her breath so she would not cry out, 'Stop it.'

'Laura, dear, you are such fun to be with. I should not say anything against Janice for she is Sir Henry's daughter and will be my wife one day, but she is a very quiet girl, not at all my style really, though I daresay we will rub along somehow. Now you are different. You don't mind a bit of fun and games and it is not just because you are the nurserymaid. I do not take advantage of the maids and I don't mind you knowing it. I look far higher for my pleasures and at the moment I am looking no higher than the respectable Miss Fawcett. And I have not forgotten that sweet kiss in the maze. I was denied my second one because we could hear Janice coming. May I take it now, Laura?'

Laura stood up.

'I declare it is not safe to be on my own with you, Sir Rowland. Oh, you naughty man, and just because I am wearing a low-necked dress in this warm weather. Well, just one kiss then. I think if I don't let you kiss me, you will be chasing me all round the nursery and we haven't even finished the jigsaws yet.'

Laura was scandalised at her own behaviour. Whatever is it in me that lets me behave in such a way, she was thinking. But I have got him very interested and all for the price of a kiss.

'Laura, Laura,' he was almost panting. 'Let me hold you in my arms. You were made for me. I'm damned if you weren't. What is the matter?'

'Sit down at the table quickly and do the jigsaw. I can hear footsteps on the stairs. It sounds like the children.'

'I'll have you yet,' he muttered, but he did as he was told and when Janice came in with the children, he rose to his feet and bowed politely.

Janice looked from one to the other. Sir Rowland's colour was heightened and although Laura was looking composed, there was a twinkle of mischief in her eyes. She has been flirting again with Sir Rowland, Janice

79

thought. Whatever does she thinks she is up to?

'My dear Janice,' Sir Rowland was saying. 'Laura persuaded me to wait for you and we have been sorting out the jigsaws. Me doing a jigsaw at my age, but it is complete, Fanny, look.'

'It's the cats and dogs one,' Fanny cried. 'It has been muddled up for ages. Oh, thank you, Sir Rowland. Do unscrabble it and let me do it again.'

'Are you going to stay for luncheon, Sir Rowland?' Janice asked.

'No, I must be on my way. I came to see your father about this wretched business of the railway. They are threatening to bring it through Thornton-le-Moor, you know. I am sorry to have missed you but it was a pleasure to see Miss Laura.'

'Yes, I am pleased that she was here. Do come again tomorrow and we can walk together while the fine weather lasts.'

Sir Rowland left and Janice turned to Laura, hugging her round the waist.

'You are flirting with him again, I can tell it by your expression. What are you up to, Laura? No, you needn't tell me, but I am beginning to get suspicious.'

Laura laughed.

'I think you will soon know about it, Janice, and be as cool as you like with Sir Rowland. And that is all I will say.'

'Oh, Laura, it was a good day when you came here, even if you are playing tricks on me. You are very welcome to Sir Rowland, you know.'

'I don't want him, Janice, thank you very much. I will go and prepare for luncheon.'

In spite of their arrangements for Laura to have her meals in the nursery with the children, she had ended up joining the family at the dining table, while a maid joined the children in the nursery. It had been useless for her to protest for Sir Henry and Lady Dorothy had ended up treating her as though she was a sister to Janice.

As she reached the dining-room that day, she met up with Aubrey. He looked out of temper and she soon learned why.

'I've just met Sir Rowland, strutting out of the house like the cat that's swallowed the cream. And do you know what he said to me?'

'I've no idea, Mr Aubrey,' Laura replied immediately.

'"Good day to you, Aubrey," he said and very bumptious he was, too. "What a splendid young woman your Miss Fawcett is, damn if she ain't." What the devil are you about, Miss Laura? You are not a lady of Sir Rowland's stamp. You don't even like him, do you?'

'No, I do not like him. I think I have told you so before. But it amuses me to keep him out of Janice's way, poor girl. I would do anything to rescue her from his grasp, so

81

please shut your eyes to my behaviour.'

She looked at the dubious expression on his face and thought she had better try and change the vexed subject.

'You know that your parents spoil me, Mr Aubrey. They treat me almost as another daughter, and I am supposed to be the nurserymaid.'

'You are an excellent nurserymaid as far as I can see. I have never seen the children so well-behaved and they are interested in everything. They even wanted me to tell them if the railway was going to spoil Fox Wood, and had I ever seen a locomotive, was it very dirty, did it go very fast?'

'They are the railway passengers of the future, I think, Mr Aubrey.'

'You are right. Are you always right? As for the game you are playing with Sir Rowland Hutton, I am not sure that I approve.'

'Perhaps I will marry Sir Rowland and leave Janice and Hugh to live happily ever after.'

She found her arm held in a tight grip. She almost winced, yet Aubrey's iron grip did not offend her as much as Sir Rowland's smooth caress.

'You will not marry Sir Rowland,' he snapped.

'And who says so?'

'I do and don't ask me why because I don't know. All I know is that I would rather hold you in my arms than see you in his.'

And with this astonishing statement, he left her standing and went into the dining-room.

CHAPTER SIX

On Laura's next free day, she took the dog-cart and went to visit Jane, James and her mother in Helmsley. It was a warm day but cloudy and she had put a cape in the cart in case of showers.

Her sister and family lived in a comfortable house not far from the church and as Laura entered it that day, she knew that it would never have suited her to have lived with her mother and Jane in such close confines. But Mrs Fawcett had fitted well into the household and she loved being able to help Jane with the children.

Laura knew that James was a man of substance and well-connected in the area. His father had been Sir Lawrence Tempest and Lord Benfold was his godfather. She did not say so to Jane or her mother, but she had come to Helmsley especially to seek James out. She was told that he was down in the orchard overseeing the picking of the plums. There were extensive gardens at the back of the house and James was proud of the vegetables and fruit he produced.

Laura found him easily and was amused to see him dressed in the same fashion as his gardeners. I wish I could find a James, she found herself thinking, and for an instant, the

84

face of Mr Aubrey Greene flashed across her mind's eye and she called herself foolish.

'Laura, how lovely to see you. We are picking our early plums. They are usually a little later up here in the north but the good weather has brought them forward this year. Did you want to see me about something? I hope all is well at Roxby Hall. We keep hearing stories of the railway. Come back to the vegetable garden where I have a convenient seat and you can tell me all about it.'

Dear James, Laura thought, as they sat down. I am sure you are going to be able to help me.

'Now to what do I owe the pleasure of this visit, Laura? Are you sure you don't want to spend the time with your mother and Jane?'

Laura shook her head.

'No, James, neither of them knows this but I came over especially to see you and to ask if you can help me.'

'I certainly will if I can,' he replied instantly and with a smile. 'Tell me about it.'

'James, it was you who found the post at Roxby Hall for me and I have told you a little about me being a companion to Sir Henry's daughter, Janice, as well as being the nurserymaid. There is an arranged marriage for Janice with Sir Rowland Hutton of Thornton-le-Moor, and it is not to her taste. He is not a young man and is of questionable morals, but that is only part of the tale. She is in love with the curate of Ellerton, and he loves her. He is young and his name is Hugh Rutherford, but his salary as a curate is very low and he can hardly support himself let alone a wife and family. Janice is prepared to wait for him but all the time she is under pressure to marry Sir Rowland and . . . why are you laughing at me?' she asked. 'I am very serious.'

'I'm sorry, Laura dear, I am not laughing. It is just that I know exactly what you are going to ask me. Do I know of anyone who has in their power a suitable living for Hugh?'

'Am I so transparent?' she demanded and then she, too, laughed. 'Yes, that is just what I was going to ask you. Do you, James, do you know of anyone? I would prefer it to be somewhere near Thirsk or Helmsley.'

'I daresay you would, Laura,' he said dryly. 'I believe it is true that there are fewer young men going into the church these days. It seems to be all the rage to go into politics or read for the law. It so happens that I know of two opportunities. One I think you will consider too far distant. It is at the other side of Ripon, but I do know that Lord Garfield of The Grange, at North Hetherington, needs someone to fill the vacancy at South Hetherington which is the neighbouring village.'

'But that is this side of Northallerton,'

Laura said. 'It would be splendid. Oh, James, do you think you could help?'

'Yes, Laura. I will write to Lord Garfield and put forward your young man's name. I will take your word for it that he is suitable but, of course, it would all have to be decided in an interview. Come into the house with me now and we will put together a letter and it will go in this afternoon's post. But, Laura . . .'

James sounded puzzled.

'What is it, James?'

'It is all very well getting a suitable living for young Hugh, but how do you dispose of the other gentleman?'

'I have it all in hand, James. He happens to be making overtures to me and I hope I can carry off my scheme successfully.'

He laughed.

'I do believe that you are up to no good, Laura. Don't get left with Sir Rowland. I believe I know of his character and it is nothing good. Neither do I want you to lose your position with Sir Henry and Lady Dorothy, though you could always come to us here even if it is a bit of a squash!'

Laura reached up and kissed him.

'Don't worry, I will not bother you. You have been good enough to take Mama in.'

'But she is most welcome, Laura, and such a help to Jane. It is a pleasure to have her with us.'

Back at the house, the letter was duly

written and went off with the mail coach that afternoon.

It took less than a week to have Hugh on his way to discuss the matter with Lord Garfield, and only a few hours for him to procure the position at South Hetherington. There was a solid, old vicarage which Hugh knew that Janice would love and he rode back to Ellerton a happy, young man. He was certain of Janice's favourable reaction but he was dubious about her parents. Would they insist on the arrangement with Sir Rowland or would they let her go to the man she loved?

In the end, he found that it was Laura he had to come to an agreement with and not Janice. He was on his way to Roxby Hall the day after his interview at North Hetherington when he saw a horse being galloped furiously in his direction. He reigned in and waited as soon as he saw that it was Laura.

'Laura,' he called out. 'The greatest news! I have procured the living at South Hetherington. I am on my way to tell Janice for it means we will be able to marry if her parents will agree.'

Laura did not dismount but faced Hugh from Whisky's back.

'Hugh, I have something to tell you and you may not be very pleased.'

'Is it to do with Sir Rowland?' he asked her.

'Yes, it is. How did you guess?'

'Laura, it is obvious. I am now in a position

to offer for Janice, but Sir Henry might still prefer her to be married to a baronet and not to a country vicar. Somehow I have to convince them.'

'Hugh, listen to me. Would you give me one day to get Sir Rowland out of the way for you?'

He stared at her.

'Laura, what are you saying? You are never going to murder the man?'

Laura laughed.

'No, Hugh, I don't mean murder, far from it. I have been playing a game with Sir Rowland and this has to be the last scene. I will say nothing more. Just keep your news to yourself for today, and come to Roxby Hall at this time tomorrow and I hope with all my heart that Sir Henry will welcome you with open arms. Do you have to see him today on railway business?"

'No. There is no sign of any surveyors yet. They are probably still going over Mr Gregson's land. But, Laura, I really do not know what to make of you for you are being very mysterious.'

'But you trust me?'

'Yes, I trust you, Laura. You have shown nothing but kindness and friendship to Janice and myself. And I will be patient with my good news and let you work your magic spell on Sir Rowland. But you won't marry him yourself, will you? I am afraid that there are tales about him which obviously have not reached the ears of Sir Henry.'

'I believe you to be right and I will be very cautious. I will be on my way now. I have to talk to Janice and I will be careful not to say anything about your appointment. That is your own special piece of news for tomorrow.'

At Roxby Hall, after a luncheon with just Sir Henry, Lady Dorothy and Janice—Aubrey was away on business—Laura spoke to Janice before they reached the nursery.

'Janice, I have something very particular which I want to do this afternoon and it will take the whole afternoon. Would you take the children out on your own just for once? I would not ask you if it was not important.'

Janice looked at her.

'Are you up to mischief again, Laura? You won't go to Fox Wood, will you? I'm not at all sure when we expect the surveyors.'

Laura was able to reply with perfect truth.

'I promise I won't go near Fox Wood, and I also promise to tell you all about it afterwards.'

She went to her room and chose her brightest and flimsiest summer dress. It was of pink Indian muslin and had been purchased for a party. The frilled collar which only just covered her shoulders, was low cut and in those days of modestly-high necks, Laura should have worn it with a chemisette but she deliberately failed to put it in its place.

She sat in the dog-cart with Whisky's reins in her hands and set off on her journey to

Holly Grange to see Sir Rowland! She was so determined on it that it did not enter her head that he might not be at home. As it was, when she arrived, she was told that Sir Rowland was sitting down in the summerhouse with the morning paper. Laura gave a sigh of relief. It was just as though fate had set the stage for her and she was so pleased that it did not occur to her that she was being very indiscreet.

The maid took her along the gravel path which led to a small group of birch trees under which had been built a wooden summerhouse with glass windows. It not being a sunny day, the glazed doors were shut and the maid gave a sharp tap. Sir Rowland appeared and when he saw Laura, he gave a beam of delight and held out his arms to her. Laura faced him politely.

'Sir Rowland, forgive me for intruding upon you, but I had to come this way on an errand for Sir Henry and I thought to call and see if you were at home, also to learn if you had any more news from the railway company.'

'Be damned to the railway company if you will excuse me, Laura. It is delightful to see you. And are you on your own?'

'Yes, I am. I didn't want to bring children all this way today, so Janice has taken them out for me.'

'A good girl, Janice, a very good girl.'

He was holding the door open and reached out to take her hand to draw her into the summerhouse beside him.

'Do come and talk to me. This is a splendid surprise.'

Laura knew that it was Sir Rowland's habit to talk endlessly and she said very little but leaned forward in her chair so that he could not fail to see that her dress was daringly open at the neck. She knew it was most improper but it was all done very deliberately.

'My dear Laura, you have me in a flutter, indeed you have, and here we are, alone and quite private. What could be more romantic? And do you know what I would like to do? I would like to plant just a little kiss in the neck of your dress. It is so inviting. No, do not draw back, I mean you no harm, no more than a little gesture of tenderness. Janice would never allow such a liberty, but, Laura, you are so different, so deliciously different.'

'Oh, Sir Rowland, you know you are a great flatterer. I don't know when I heard such nonsense. Janice is a much prettier girl than I am.'

'Janice might be prettier, Laura, but she is much too modest for my liking. Come and sit on my lap. Janice would never do such a thing.'

'Sir Rowland, what wicked things you say. No, no, you cannot pull me up to sit on your lap. That is most unladylike, indeed I think it is improper.'

Laura knew that her voice was trilling and that she had never behaved so badly, but it was all going so much better than she could have imagined.

'Oh, there, you have caught me and I must say that it is quite a nice sensation to be on the lap of such a fine gentleman as yourself. Well, just one kiss then.'

She felt his lips on the flesh above her breast and shuddered. Then his hand reached for her skirts and she felt a sense of panic.

'Sir Rowland, you are behaving disgracefully. I feel insulted, I really do. A kiss is one thing but you must not . . . no, you cannot . . .'

'Laura, you are the most tempting, young woman I have met for a very long time. Come up to my chambers with me. No one will know. Laura!' he cried out suddenly.

For Laura had jumped from his lap and stood facing him, pulling her dress back straight.

'Now I know what you are. There is a wicked word which ladies never use, but I am only the nurserymaid and I can say it. You are a lecher, and it is no wonder that poor Janice detests you. She will never marry you because the Reverend Hugh Rutherford has got the incumbency of South Hetherington and Janice will be able to marry him. I have found out just what you are like and I will warn Sir Henry. I will say goodbye.'

Laura walked to the door, her eyes blazing, but his words followed her.

'And you are nothing but a harlot and a

Jezebel!'

Laura heard no more and was almost overcome, but she managed to reach the dog-cart and start off on her way back to Roxby Hall.

It went according to plan, she was telling herself, but I am ashamed. How could I possibly have behaved in such a way? But now I do know that he is a loathsome creature and I have saved Janice. There is only one more thing to be done and I must go straight back to Sir Henry and Lady Dorothy.

At Roxby Hall, she was lucky to find Janice in the nursery with the children and Sir Henry and Lady Dorothy in the drawing-room with Aubrey. She could have wished that Aubrey was not there but nothing was going to stop her in this final attempt to help Janice out of her difficulties. She did not yet know if Hugh had come over to see Janice that afternoon.

Lady Dorothy looked at her.

'Why, Laura, you look flustered about something and your dress, Laura, it is quite open at the neck and not at all proper. Where have you been?'

Laura drew in a deep breath. She could see that Aubrey was looking at her with suspicious, frowning eyes.

'I will be quite open and honest with you, Sir Henry, and Lady Dorothy, Mr Aubrey. Since I have been at Roxby Hall and in the company of Janice most of the time, I have discovered that she has become very distressed on the subject of her marriage to Sir Rowland Hutton. At the same time, I have heard servants' hall gossip about him and I did not like the sound of it. I know that to you, it is a very respectable match for Janice and I honour you for wanting to do your best for her.'

She paused, found that she had their full attention, then launched on to the difficult part of her story.

'I decided I would go and see Sir Rowland and try to find out if the rumours were true. I had my own suspicions because he has been most familiar with me. That is where I have been this afternoon. I have just returned from Holly Grange. Lady Dorothy, Janice cannot marry that man. He behaved in the most improper way to mc and whcn I protested he said that I was the most tempting, young woman he had met for a very long time. Those were his very words. I cannot in all modesty tell you what happened next, but when he asked me to go up to his chambers I am afraid I lost my temper with him and said he was not fit to marry Janice. He is not, Lady Dorothy, truly he is not.'

She paused briefly for breath then continued.

'I am in no position to tell you what to do and I have been very forward for Janice's sake, but I beg you not to insist on this alliance. She has an admirable young suitor in Hugh Rutherford and he is sure to get a good living somewhere sooner or later.'

She stopped and looked at Aubrey, startled at the angry look in his eyes.

'I am sure Mr Aubrey will agree with me.'

'Yes, I do,' he answered her but the words were almost a grunt.

Sir Henry got up and went over to Laura.

'Laura, I appreciate what you have tried to do for Janice and I hope you have not sullied your own reputation. I ask you now to go up to the nursery while we discuss what you have told us. Bring Janice down in about ten minutes before we sit down to dinner.'

Laura almost ran upstairs, relieved to have the awkward scene over. She had found it more difficult than she had thought it would be and put this down to the fact that Aubrey had been in the room. But these motives were forgotten as soon as she saw Janice.

'Laura, you are back, oh, thank goodness. I have such news for you. Hugh came to see me and he is to be the vicar of South Hetherington. It is not far from here and there is a lovely vicarage. Oh, if only I could get Mama and Papa to forget about Sir Rowland, then Hugh and I would be able to marry. I am almost afraid to tell them in case they insist on the arrangement with Sir Rowland. Whatever shall I do?'

Laura kissed her and knew her moment of

triumph had come. All the impropriety of her visit to Holly Grange had been worth while.

'We will get Patsy to give the children their supper and you can go down and see your parents. You just have time before dinner.'

'You will come with me?'

'Yes, I will come with you.'

Sir Henry was at his most serious and kindest when they joined them. He took Janice by the shoulders and looked at her searchingly.

'My dear girl, we want to tell you that we have learned facts about Sir Rowland Hutton's lifestyle which have made us reconsider the arrangements we made with him. If you do not wish for the match, I will go and see him tomorrow morning. As for the Reverend Hugh Rutherford, I consider him to be a very respectable and responsible young gentleman, and we would not oppose a marriage between the two of you. We would only ask that you would wait until he has a better position.'

'Oh, Papa.'

Janice kissed him and then threw her arms around her mother's neck.

'What good parents you are. Everything has happened today, for Hugh came over this afternoon to tell me that he is to be the vicar of South Hetherington. And I thought I hardly dare tell you in case you insisted on the marriage with Sir Rowland. What can I say?'

Lady Dorothy smiled at Laura who shook her head.

97

'I am very happy for you, Janice, and I expect Hugh will come and ask your father's permission to address you tomorrow. You will certainly have our blessing. Now let us go into dinner and we can talk about it.'

Laura was very quiet during the meal which was formal and lengthy and consisted of four courses before the dessert was served. She was conscious that Aubrey seemed very displeased though he made an obvious effort to hide his feelings for Janice's sake.

'How did Hugh hear of the position at South Hetherington, Janice?' he asked, sounding suspicious.

'He had a letter from Lord Garfield to invite him for an interview. Apparently Lord Garfield had not been able to find just the person he wanted for the incumbency and he said that although Hugh was very young, he thought he would suit the country parish admirably.'

The ladies returned to the drawing-room while Lord Henry and Aubrey partook of their port. When they did at last join the ladies, Aubrey walked straight across the room to Laura.

'Come into the garden with me,' he said to her.

His tone was so compelling that Laura got up and did his bidding.

CHAPTER SEVEN

It was with some trepidation that Laura followed Aubrey into the garden, then she became amused as he went right down to the seat in the orchard.

He does not want anyone to hear what he has to say to me, she thought.

'Sit down,' he ordered. 'I want to talk to you privately.'

'Yes, Mr Aubrey,' she murmured.

He shot a look of suspicion at her.

'It is no use pretending meekness,' he said. 'Your behaviour has been far from meek and you know very well that I am angry with you.'

'You have no right to be angry with me, sir,' she replied sharply.

'I have no right in relation to yourself even if you are the family nurserymaid, but I do have a right in my sister's interests.'

This stung her.

'But, Mr Aubrey, everything I did was in Janice's interest. It really did hurt me that she was unable to marry Hugh. He is not only a very nice and proper young man, he is from a good family and is very respectable. It was only his lowly status which was against him.'

'And what had you to do with that, might I ask, ma'am? I have a feeling that Hugh's preferment to South Hetherington did not come out of the blue.'

Laura gave a chuckle then. Perhaps he was not going to be as angry as she had feared.

'It happened more easily than I had expected. I paid a visit to my brotherin-law, Mr James Tempest of Helmsley, as I knew he had influence in the county. As it happened, he knew of two vacant livings in North Yorkshire, but we applied first to Lord Garfield who has the patronage of South Hetherington. It was the nearest one, you see.'

'Yes, I do see,' he said grimly.

'As you now know, Lord Garfield was delighted with Hugh and had no hesitation in giving him the living. You have seen for yourself how pleased and happy Janice is.'

'And are you blaming me for not taking any previous action on behalf of my sister?'

Laura turned and looked at him genuinely puzzled.

'Mr Aubrey, of course I do not blame you. I know that you did not approve of the match between Janice and Sir Rowland, but how were you to know what a despicable man he really was?'

Suddenly his hands shot out and he gripped her by the shoulders.

'And that brings me to the second part of these proceedings. Sir Rowland Hutton. How did you find out what the man was really like? Did you tell my parents the whole story? In other words, and I do not apologise for my language, did you take Sir Rowland as a lover?'

Even Laura was shocked. She knew she had acted improperly but that Aubrey should think that she had gone to such wicked lengths! She wrenched herself away from his strong hands. She stood up and with the back of her hand, she struck him violently across his face.

'How dare you! How dare you!' she screamed at him.

His reply was to grasp her round the waist and pull her back on to the seat. He forced her back, bent over and kissed her viciously. Laura could not move and went rigid as she suffered the insult of the kiss. Then she felt him relax and his lips became more gentle, and what had started in violence ended in passionate tenderness. Her arms went round his neck, and the kiss continued. At last, he lifted his head.

'Laura, my goodness,' he said and she could tell he was shocked.

Slowly, she recovered from her own stirred emotions and realised the truth of her feelings for him. And yet she sat up and looked at him bitterly.

'You are no better than Sir Rowland,' she said.

'No, Laura, you must listen to me.'

'I will not. You gentlemen are all the same. You want only one thing.'

'Laura, do not speak in such a way. It does

101

not become you, or are you really the trollop you must have pretended to be for Sir Rowland's sake?'

She glared at him.

'You are determined to think the worst of me. Yes, I did lead Sir Rowland on and he did kiss me, but that was all, do you hear? That was all. When I went to visit him at Holly Grange, he was most familiar which was what I expected but when he asked me to go to his bedroom with him, I knew I had truly found him out. I turned on him then and told him what I thought of him and assured him that he would never marry Miss Janice Greene.'

Aubrey had not spoken and sat with his face buried in his hands.

'So now, Mr Aubrey, you know the whole truth. I deliberately played the hussy for Janice's sake for I could not bear that she should go through such indignities. Janice is a good girl and has found her true love. I am a wicked girl and if you mean me to lose my place, then I will say goodbye to you and give in my notice to your parents. Is that your wish and intention in bringing me here?'

He lifted his head and looked at her.

'Laura, go away from me for I am tempted by you just as Sir Rowland was. I thought to have my passions in hand, but I have behaved no better than he and certainly not as a gentleman should behave. I was jealous, do you hear? Yes, you may stare at me for I do not know what it means myself. I have to believe that you acted the hussy for Janice's sake and you have made her very happy. I thank you for that and I apologise for the slur on your name. And you have made me realise that I could have done more for her, but Sir Rowland has always been on the politest terms with me.'

He was silent for a moment, as though he was trying to work out why it had been Laura who had come to his sister's aid and not himself.

'I believe that I am so enmeshed in this business of the railway that I did not even give Janice and Sir Rowland a thought. All I have been able to think about is how to save Fox Wood. It seemed to be the most important thing in the world to me. My own sister's happiness seemed as nothing and I am ashamed. So, yes, go away from me, but do not leave us. My parents love you, Janice needs you and the children adore you.'

He took her hand in his.

'I promise not to think badly of you and will believe that you led Sir Rowland into impropriety only for Janice's sake. You played the part of the hussy and played it well, but I know that is not the real Miss Laura.'

She smiled then.

'Sir Rowland called me a harlot and a Jezebel.'

He lifted her hand to his lips.

'And so you are, but only for me.'

'Mr Aubrey.'

'Miss Laura, go away from me.'

Laura went back to the house and straight up to her room without seeing anyone. She had a lot to think about, and what she thought of most of all was Aubrey's kiss and how the savageness of it had turned to sweetness.

I must forget it, she told herself. Mr Aubrey is not for me. I am only the nurserymaid.

But her thoughts did not finish there. It would be very easy to love Mr Aubrey but she tried to dismiss the thought from her mind.

The following morning, everything seemed to happen at once. Hugh came to Roxby Hall to see Sir Henry and received permission to address himself to Janice. The engagement was announced and Lady Dorothy insisted that they must have an engagement party. On top of this, a letter arrived from Sir Rowland saying that he withdrew his suit and was intending to go on a six months' visit to a cousin who lived in the Scottish Highlands and that he would stay there for the shooting season. They would have to manage the railway business without him.

In the midst of this excitement and jollity, a serious-looking Aubrey came into the drawing-room to announce that a message had come from Francis Gregson to say that surveyors had measured his land and were now on their way to Ellerton and Roxby Hall. They were only a few fields away from the blighted cottages and Fox Wood. He would send men from his estate to join those of Sir Henry's.

Sir Henry, Aubrey and Hugh went off, leaving a worried-looking Lady Dorothy talking about firearms and violence. Laura had brought the children downstairs ready for their morning outing and she tried to reassure Janice and her mother.

'Lady Dorothy, I am sure they will be able to hold sensible talks and settle things peaceably. Try not to worry.'

Lady Dorothy gave a wan smile.

'You don't know my husband, Laura, dear, or Aubrey for that matter. They are fiercely proud of their inheritance and will go to any lengths to protect Fox Wood from the railway company.'

Laura was reminded of Aubrey's shot at the first surveyor who had appeared and secretly thought that it all might end up as a rough affair, but she was not going to say this.

'I cannot see Sir Henry or Mr Aubrey or Hugh, for that matter, going around with shotguns under their arms, Lady Dorothy. Try not to worry.'

Laura and Janice had decided to ride that morning. It was a favourite pastime and Samuel, Fanny and Jessica all had ponies. Sir Henry insisted that one of the stable-boys always accompanied them and they all enjoyed their rides. As they walked round to the stables, Aubrey came up quickly on his own horse.

'Where are you going?' he asked shortly.

Laura looked at him, thinking he looked worried.

It was Janice who replied.

'We are going for a short ride with the children on their ponies. We usually take one of the stable lads with us, but I expect you will need all the help you can get. You do not object to us going out? We won't go near the wood.'

'As you have promised the children, you had better go, but on no account go in the direction of Ellerton. You can keep in the area of Breckenbrough. There will be no trouble there. Just keep out of the way, that is all I ask of you. We have enough trouble on our hands as it is.'

'Have you seen the surveyors coming yet?' Laura asked.

'No. We have Father's telescope but there is no sign of anyone. I came back to warn you to stay out of the way and I'll be off again now.'

He dug in his heels, gave a flash of his whip and galloped off in the direction of Fox Wood. Janice looked after him as she helped the children on to their ponies.

'He looks worried, Laura. That is not like Aubrey. Can they really chop the wood down to make way for a railway? It seems all wrong.'

'It is going on all over the country, I am

afraid. Most landowners dislike the idea of a noisy and dirty steam engine going across their land.'

'I would agree with that,' Janice said, 'but you seem to be in favour of the railways.'

'I am in favour of the kind of progress which will make it easier to travel from one place to another. Our roads are poor but they are so crowded with slow carriages and farm wagons. Everything has to be carried on the roads and it would be much quicker and more efficient to be put on to a goods train.'

'You are very forward-looking, Laura.'

Laura smiled.

'I expect it comes with living in a town. I have grown up seeing Thirsk choked with traffic on market days and this latest line they are making will open the railway to Thirsk.'

She paused as she jumped up on her mare.

'What I don't understand, Janice, is why the railway company will insist on such a straight line. If only they curved a little in some places, it would avoid a lot of argument and legal battles with landowners.'

'You are thinking of Fox Wood,' Janice said.

'Yes, I suppose I am. But let us set off and enjoy our ride and forget about the railway for a little while.'

They let the children's ponies ride on ahead and followed side by side so that they could talk together as they went along.

They were still riding in the parkland on the

far side of Fox Wood and they could see Breckenbrough Hall in the distance. It was Janice who first spotted the men.

'Laura, look,' Janice said, pointing. 'By that clump of fir trees. There are some men and they are coming in this direction.'

Laura paused and looked ahead.

'Perhaps they are the gamekeepers from Breckenbrough looking out for the surveyors, though it is strange, because Aubrey said that there were no complications at Breckenbrough.

She broke off and stared in the direction of the slowly-moving group of men.

'Janice, they are carrying things. It looks like surveyors' staffs and theodolites and the things I can't quite make out must be the chains. I know that a chain is a measure of twenty-two yards but Aubrey told me that they use links of chains of the exact length for their measuring.'

She watched for several minutes, then with a sudden decision spurred herself and her horse into action.

'There is no doubt about it, Janice. They are making for Fox Wood from the opposite direction. Your father and Aubrey were expecting them to approach from Ellerton. At this rate, the measuring of the wood will be done before Sir Henry even knows that the men are here. I'm going, Janice. I am going to the other side of Fox Wood to warn them. I might be just in time.'

'You cannot, Laura. Aubrey would be very

cross. He said that we were not to go near Fox Wood.'

'It won't be the first time that Aubrey has been cross with me. That bothers me very little. It is Fox Wood that I care about. Janice, take the children straight back to Roxby Hall. I'm off.'

'You are nothing but a hot-head, Laura.'

'I've been called worse than that. Take care how you go. Goodbye.'

Janice watched as Laura went off at full gallop in the direction of the wood and she saw that she reached it a long time before the group of men on foot were anywhere near. Dear Laura, Janice thought, I think our lives have changed since she came to us. I wish that Aubrey liked her a little better. It would be lovely to have her as a sister.

As Laura came into the open at the other side of Fox Wood, she reined in with something of a shock. Standing in a group, some of them with staves and cudgels, were about fifty men. Farthest away from her and carrying shotguns, she could pick out Mr Gregson and Hugh, Sir Henry and Aubrey. She galloped up to them and jumped down to confront them, completely ignoring Aubrey's furious words.

'Laura, I told you not come near the wood. Cannot you see that it is dangerous? We are all prepared to meet the surveyors with force if necessary as soon as they appear from

Ellerton. Go back immediately.'

Laura took no notice of these words but addressed herself to Sir Henry who was not looking pleased.

'I have ridden to tell you, Sir Henry, that Janice and I have just seen a group of surveyors approaching the wood from the opposite side. I sent Janice home with the children and came to warn you. If you station yourself here, they will have measured the wood before you are even aware of their presence. You need to be through the wood quickly to meet them before they reach the other side.'

He looked at her as though stunned that a young woman in his employ should have the temerity to come and give him orders, but it was Aubrey who spoke.

'Laura, are you sure?'

She nodded vehemently.

'They were carrying theodolites, staffs and chains. I did not waste any time coming to warn you. You will have to be quick to catch them, though I came as fast as I could through the wood and . . .'

But she got no further. Aubrey turned to his father.

'This explains why we have not seen them coming from the direction of Ellerton. Shall we go, Father?'

Sir Henry shouted his orders and the whole group of men and boys were swallowed up in

110

the wood as they ran forward. Laura watched them and decided what to do next.

I'm not missing this, she told herself, and turned back and galloped the length of the wood to arrive just as Sir Henry and Aubrey emerged from the trees to confront the surveyors.

She tethered her horse and walked closer, trying not to be seen for she knew it was no place for a lady, even a lady turned nurserymaid. As she crept nearer, she could hear the tense argument. Sir Henry was silent and it was Aubrey and the deputation leader, William Fortescue, whose voices were raised in anger.

'Some of the trees in this wood have stood here for five hundred years and they are not going to be felled to make way for a railway. You will have to find another route.'

'I am afraid that is not possible,' the surveyor replied and Laura thought that he was reasonably polite.

'And why not, might I ask?'

The words from Aubrey were shot as from a gun.

'The line from Thirsk to Northallerton is direct and straight and we have no need for cuttings or tunnels.'

'But it would pass through this wood?'

'That is correct.'

'But it cannot pass through the wood if you are not able to survey it.'

'You would try to stop us then, Mr Greene?'

'That is our purpose in coming here today,' Aubrey replied solidly.

Mr Fortescue could not keep the curiosity from his voice.

'And how did you learn that we would approach the wood from the Breckenbrough side?'

Laura held her breath, but Aubrey's anger was rising and she could tell that he was not going to admit that his intelligence had come from his mother's nurserymaid.

'We have our ways of finding out these things. We happen to know about some of the tricks you use to gain access to a property, like firing guns in a different place so that our men and gamekeepers rush there and leave you free to do the surveying.'

'You are well-informed, sir, but you will please note that there has been no firing today.'

'Not yet,' Aubrey grunted.

'So you are going to let us into the wood?'

'We are not going to let you anywhere near the wood. I have fifty men in the trees waiting to stop you.'

Aubrey stepped forward and in what Laura saw was a futile and angry gesture, pushed the surveyor away from him.

'Be off with you and take your men with you.'

'I will do no such thing. If I have to fight you

112

with bare knuckles, we will gain entry to the wood.'

'You would not dare,' Aubrey shouted.

'I certainly will dare and you can take that for a starter,' and the surveyor, with clenched fists, hit Aubrey hard on the side of the head. Aubrey went reeling with the force of the blow.

'Aubrey,' Sir Henry shouted.

Laura, without knowing she had moved, ran forward and placed herself between the two men.

'Stop it, you fools,' she yelled out and did not recognise her own voice. 'Haven't you the wit to see that there is a peaceable way out of all this? Yes, you may look at me. I am Sir Henry's nurserymaid and even I can see that you can avoid Fox Wood with no trouble at all. You don't need to start the track in the middle of Thirsk. You could take it a little to the west and with only a slight curve you would avoid the Ellerton cottages, skirt Fox Wood and not only that, you will avoid going too close to Sir Rowland Hutton's house at Thornton-le-Moor.'

Her voice tailed off as she felt a strong grip on her arm and saw that Sir Henry had stepped forward, looking very angry.

'Miss Fawcett, I do not know what you are doing here but I am ashamed that one of my servants should behave in such a forward manner. Go straight back to the house, pack your things and await me there.'

Laura felt the tears sting her eyes and she looked at Aubrey. He was staring at her with a mixture of admiration and condemnation in his eyes. Then she saw herself as an impetuous fool and she turned and ran to her horse, jumped up and galloped back to Roxby Hall in no more than a few minutes. You fool! You behaved like a common village woman in front of all those men, she told herself. What you said might have made sense, but it was not your place to say it. And now there will be fighting amongst them and Sir Henry has ordered you to leave.

She went in search of Janice then, and threw herself into the girl's arms.

'Laura, what is it? What have you done? You never ever cry about anything.'

Janice was looking dismayed and held on tightly to Laura as Laura told her what had happened. She received the expected rebuke.

'But you couldn't have said all that in front of Papa and Aubrey and the surveyor when they were arguing. It wasn't ladylike, Laura. You know better than that. Why ever did you do it?'

'They made me so angry, Janice. It suddenly burst upon me that there was such an easy solution and all they would talk about was fighting over the wood and there I was shouting at them. Your poor papa, he was horrified and . . . Janice, he has told me to

114

pack my things. I am dismissed.'

'Oh, no, Laura, I cannot believe it.'

'It is my own fault, but at least I have got you and Hugh safely together. I have achieved something while I have been here and I have been so happy. Now I must go and pack and wait until your papa comes back.'

Laura paused.

'Janice, would you go and tell Lady Dorothy? I fear that Sir Henry is very angry and I think we had better warn her.'

CHAPTER EIGHT

When Laura was finally called downstairs to see Sir Henry, she entered the drawing-room nervously and was upset to see that Lady Dorothy had been crying. Sir Henry rose instantly, glanced at his wife, then walked towards Laura. He looked very put out and very serious.

'Come into the library, Miss Fawcett,' he said abruptly. 'My wife is very upset at your behaviour, and also, I must tell you, because we are losing you. The things I have to say to you are best said between the two of us on our own.'

In the library, Laura was motioned into the chair in front of Sir Henry's desk.

'I need not tell you,' he began stiffly, 'that your actions in front of Mr Fortescue and his surveyors were out of place to say the least of it. Only a female of a certain class would have dared to intrude in such a gathering, and that is not to mention the danger of the situation. I brought you here as my nurserymaid because I was sorry for you in your position after your father's death. And also because I thought you would be a good influence on my children and on Janice.'

He paused and looked at her soberly.

'Janice has certainly benefited from your

116

presence here in that you brought to our attention the unsuitable character of Sir Rowland Hutton. I now find that I wonder how you were able to obtain that information. I will not ask you for it as it is in the past and both Lady Dorothy and I are pleased to see Janice so happy with Hugh Rutherford.'

Then he got up and walked round to her. Laura felt tiny, as though she had been reduced to a little girl again, but Sir Henry was magnanimous.

'I am sorry to lose you, Laura. Until today you have brought nothing but light and happiness to this house. But you must realise that I cannot keep you as a nurserymaid, a young woman who had the effrontery to interfere in what was an affair meant only for gentlemen and their estate workers. And now I must tell you that because I have had to dismiss you without notice, I intend to give you your salary for the year. I will bid you good-day.'

Laura stood up. Her heart felt as though it was made of stone.

'I do not wish for any payment, thank you, Sir Henry. Please, will you give my apologies to Lady Dorothy? I will go and say goodbye to Janice and the children and be on my way to Helmsley.'

She went up the stairs slowly. She had missed luncheon and she felt empty not only in her stomach but in her heart. I should have known better, she was telling herself bitterly. Gentlemen do not like their business affairs to be interrupted and certainly not by a woman. I only said what I thought was sensible and practical. Now I shall have to leave Roxby Hall without even knowing if Fox Wood was saved.

Janice was standing anxiously at the nursery door and she called over her shoulder to the children that she would only be a minute, then walked across the landing to meet Laura.

'Oh, Laura, whatever has happened? Papa was shouting when he came home and I could hear Mama crying. I think she was trying to keep you here.'

Laura shook her head.

'Lady Dorothy is very upset and I dare not even go and say goodbye to her. Tell her I am sorry, won't you, Janice? Your father will not keep me here and I have to admit that I did behave foolishly. I can understand him thinking that I am a bad influence. Let me get my bags, Janice. I must hurry, to be in Helmsley in time for dinner.'

Her voice broke with emotion but bravely she went on.

'Say goodbye to the children for me. Tell them I am needed at home in Helmsley or something like that, and, Janice, I wish you and Hugh every happiness. No, please, don't see me off. It will make me cry. God bless you.'

And with these words, Laura picked up her bags, hurried down the stairs and rushed round to the stables. One of the stable lads quickly got the dogcart ready and loaded it for her and she was off. She did not even glance back at the big house, where for a few months, she had been very happy.

She tried not to think of Aubrey, but she did wonder what the outcome of the meeting between the two sides had been. I shall never know, she thought sadly. She gave Whisky her head and they were soon on their way through Thirsk and up the steep cliff at Sutton Bank before they reached Helmsley.

Laura knew this was an awkward time to arrive at Petrie Lodge as the family would be sure to be just about to sit down for dinner. They would bombard her with questions when all she wanted to do was to have a quiet think about her situation and what she was to do next. She also wanted to have a quiet talk with James.

She stabled Whisky and got the boy to carry her bags into the house for her. It was Jane who seized upon her.

'Laura, what a time to come, just when we are going to sit down to dinner. Oh, dear, I must ask Rhoda to lay another place and tell cook we will be one extra. I do hope she has made a big enough steak-and-kidney pudding though why I should have asked her to make that in this sultry weather . . . and your bags! Have you lost your place? I never did think that you would make a suitable nurserymaid.

119

You can stay here if you can manage with the box-room. Mama is in the guest room and the maids have all the attic bedrooms. But I daresay we can manage until you find another place. Oh, here is James. My dear, Laura has left Roxby Hall and is come to stay with us. I hope you won't object.'

Laura had stayed still, quite stunned by her sister's tirade and smiled only when James came into the room to find out why Jane was not at the dining-table. His words went to Laura's head like wine.

'Laura, dear, how nice to see you. Come and sit at the dining-table and tell us your news. Rhoda will lay another place.'

'Laura is going to stay, James. I think she has lost her place,' Jane said.

James looked at Laura sharply. Her face was strained and her eyes were sending an urgent message to him.

'Laura can tell me about it after dinner,' he said. 'We will walk in the garden. I am sure she would rather talk about it quietly and not have all of us quizzing her.'

'Yes, dear,' his wife replied. 'You are quite right. Come along, Mama will be wondering where we are.'

James managed to whisper into Laura's ear as they went into the dining-room, 'Eat a good dinner, Laura. You look as though you need it, and a glass of wine will do you good.'

Dear James, Laura thought and not for the

120

first time. However did such a nice man come to marry Jane, but I suppose that she was a pretty little thing at the time.

After dinner, James led Laura to their usual seat in the vegetable garden. She was glad to be a good distance from the house. She had said little at dinner, leaving her mama and Jane to re-organise her life for her.

'Now, young lady, you can tell me the whole. I presume there must be some good reason for you leaving Roxby Hall in such a hurry. Have you been indiscreet?'

'I am afraid I have, James, and worse,' she replied and proceeded to tell him everything that had happened at Fox Wood that day, and then telling him of the success of his help in finding a worthwhile living for Hugh.

James was silent for a long time after she had finished speaking and Laura was afraid she had angered him.

'Are you cross with me, James?' she asked tentatively.

He smiled down at her and she knew relief though she steeled herself for a lecture.

'No, Laura, I am not cross. You did your best for Janice even if you went about getting rid of Sir Rowland in a most unladylike way. And as for Fox Wood, well, I must say that I can only admire your astute summing-up of the situation and then having the courage to say what you were thinking. Sir Henry Greene would have considered it outrageous that a

121

young woman should have spoken out in such a way, but I imagine that your Mr Aubrey might take a different view.'

He looked down and could notice only the earnest, intelligent expression which he had always admired in her.

'Laura, you must remember that a woman's rôle is changing. We already have writers like Miss Austen even though with her first book she did not give her name. And don't forget that Mary Wollstonecraft wrote about the rights of women back in the last century, and it is possible that we will have a woman on the throne of England when King William dies. What is it, Laura?'

He was looking at her face which looked a little less sombre.

'James, you are the most wonderful brother a girl ever had. Here I am confessing to doing something outrageous and instead of condemning me as Sir Henry has done, you start talking about the rights of women!'

James put his arms around her affectionately.

'I love my dear Jane,' he said, 'even if she is becoming more like your mama every day, but you are different, Laura, and I admire you. Now I suppose that you are going to be asking me what you are to do next. You would not stay here with us?'

'It would not do, James. You are very kind but I think that Jane and I living together would cause dissent and I don't want to bring that to your happy home. No, I will stay only until such time as I can find a post as a governess. I won't try and play the nurserymaid again though I have enjoyed my time at Roxby Hall. It has been quite lively.'

'I think it has been too lively for your own good, Miss Laura. Do you know the outcome of your intervention at Fox Wood?' She shook her head.

'No, Mr Aubrey had not returned so I do not suppose I will ever know.'

Laura would have been interested to have been an onlooker in the scene between Mr Aubrey Greene and his father which was taking place almost at the same time as her discussion with James.

Dinner was over when Aubrey rushed into Roxby Hall. In the drawingroom, he found his father and mother and Janice. He looked round him.

'Where is Miss Laura?' he asked abruptly.

Sir Henry replied at once.

'I have dismissed her. She is on her way back to her sister's house in Helmsley. But not to worry about that, Aubrey. What has happened at Fox Wood?'

Aubrey took no notice of this last question.

'You have dismissed her?' he snapped. 'Come into the library, Father. I wish to talk to you privately.'

In the library, father and son faced each

other across the wide desk, and it was Laura whom Aubrey wished to talk about and not Fox Wood.

'Father, have I heard you all right? You have dismissed Laura because she had the courage to speak her mind?'

'It was most unladylike, Aubrey, and coming from someone I employ as a nurserymaid, it was unpardonable. I did only what was correct and Laura accepted it. She went as soon as she had packed her bags. But, Aubrey, never mind about Laura. She was a good girl but did not know her place. It was my fault for employing her in the first instance. But I want to know what happened at Fox Wood. I left you arguing the matter with Mr Fortescue.'

'Be damned to Fox Wood. I will tell you about it as soon as I have seen Laura.'

'But you cannot go chasing all the way to Helmsley at this hour of the evening, and you have missed dinner.'

Aubrey was on his way to the door, his anger showing in his dark eyes.

'I will find something to eat in the kitchen. Then I will go to bed and be off at first light to Helmsley to see Laura. There is something I must ask her.'

'But, Aubrey!'

'I will tell you that Fox Wood is saved and no more. I have more important things on my mind at the moment.'

And he was gone.

At Petrie Lodge, Laura had passed a miserable night with confused thoughts and dreams in which the huge oak at Fox Wood became muddled up with the dark eyes of Aubrey Greene. She awoke unsure of her feelings for Mr Aubrey. She felt she had lost someone who was about to become precious to her, and yet she knew in her heart of hearts that she must have lost any burgeoning love and had alienated him for ever. She must put him out of her mind.

She went downstairs to join the family at breakfast and although she would have liked to have been on her own, she offered to take Rob and Emily for a walk. They were just getting ready to go out, when there came a heavy knocking on the front door and the maid admitted Mr Aubrey Greene. Laura, standing in the entrance hall, felt that she had been struck dumb.

'Mr Aubrey!' she stammered.

'I must see you, Miss Laura, privately. Will you let me take you for a drive? I have come in the gig.'

'I was just going to take Rob and Emily for a walk.'

She turned as she heard Jane's voice behind her.

'Who is it, Laura?'

Reluctantly, Laura made the introductions.

'Jane, this is Mr Aubrey Greene of Roxby Hall. Mr Aubrey, my sister, Jane.'

Then she looked from Aubrey to Jane and made up her mind.

'Jane, Mr Aubrey has asked me to go for a drive with him but I have promised Rob and Emily . . .'

'I will take them out, Laura,' Jane interrupted without delay. 'You go with Mr Greene and I am sure I am pleased that you have come, sir. You are most welcome to come back for a luncheon after your drive with Laura.'

'Thank you, Mrs Tempest,' Aubrey said very politely, for he was not feeling in the least polite. 'Are you ready, Miss Laura?'

'Yes, of course,' Laura replied, feeling as though she was being whisked along with no thought to her own wishes.

Aubrey helped Laura up into the gig and they were obliged to sit quite closely. Laura was angry, overjoyed and uncertain at the same time. 'Mr Aubrey . . .' she started to say.

'Be quiet. We will not say anything until we are out of Helmsley. I will take you up through Carlton to the moor.'

As it happened, Laura loved this lane out of Helmsley which turned into no more than a track towards Bransdale. It had been a favourite trip as a child with her father and it seemed strange that Aubrey should have chosen it now. As they came out of the trees, the whole of Bransdale opened out before them.

126

Aubrey pulled up and, without saying a word, helped Laura down from the gig. She gave the last little jump into his arms and it was their undoing for he held her close, bent his head and kissed her. Anger and restraint were converted into pleasure in that kiss and they clung to each other in sweet passion. Slowly Laura pulled away and looked up at him. She did not know what to expect but certainly not soft words.

'I love you, Miss Laura,' he said in no more than a whisper.

But Laura shook her head and spoke out clearly.

'No, you cannot, Mr Aubrey. I have been a servant in your father's house and there can be no question of love between us. Apart from that, your father has dismissed me because of the things I said at Fox Wood. I do not regret saying them, but as he pointed out, it was a most unladylike thing to do. You must be ashamed of me.'

Aubrey took her arm and started walking towards the moor.

'Come and walk with me and we will talk as we go. I love it here and I knew you would, too,' he declared.

'You know nothing about me, Mr Aubrey,' she replied.

'I know enough of you to make me want to fall in love with you from the moment I met you. No, don't interrupt, let me have my say.

You were fascinating to me, so much like Janice to look at yet the complete opposite in character. I am fond of my sister, but in you, Laura, I knew I had found a woman to love.'

'But, Mr Aubrey, you were displeased with me and you did not behave very well. You treated me as though I really was the servant.'

Laura could feel the emotion throbbing between them and knew that she loved him just as he loved her.

'I was jealous, Laura. I did not know what had gone on between you and Sir Rowland and I did not like the thoughts I was having.'

'I did tell you the truth. I led him on quite wickedly, I know, but I had to prove what sort of man he was for Janice's sake. It did not take long for him to reveal his true colours and I suffered only one kiss for my efforts. You had no need for jealousy.'

She stopped and turned to look at him.

'But, Mr Aubrey, yesterday at Fox Wood, I still do not know what the result was. Have you saved it?'

He put his hands on her shoulders and looked at her steadily.

'Yes, Fox Wood is saved and it was your intervention which saved it.'

'You cannot mean that. Your father was very angry with me. I had not seen him angry before. I spoke out of turn, as the saying is. You must know that.'

'Laura, my dearest girl, I have never been so

proud as I was at that moment, proud of the girl I knew I loved, proud of her courage and her intelligence. You shamed us all, Laura.'

'But, Mr Aubrey . . .'

'No, dammit, stop calling me Mr Aubrey all the time. I am Aubrey to you from this moment on.'

He sounded quite put out and she smiled.

'Very well, Aubrey, but you must tell me what happened after I had gone. Did you fight? You looked as though you were going to.'

'No, we did not fight,' he told her seriously. 'Father stalked off, but I was so proud of your commonsense that I asked Mr Fortescue to get his map out. He laid it on the ground and we looked at it and he drew a new line on it, exactly in the way you had suggested, and he was satisfied. Fox Wood was saved. Do you know, Laura, that both Mr Fortescue and myself had been so concentrating on saving the wood on my part, and obtaining it on his, that neither of us had thought of the idea of re-routing it all the way from Thirsk. Why was it you thought of it and we did not?'

Laura was thoughtful.

'I think it must be something to do with the knowledge I gained of the railways when Papa invested so badly. I must say that I never thought that his imprudence would come to my aid one day! Also my home was in Thirsk so I took a different view of it all. You could

129

only think of Fox Wood. If you knew me better, you would realise that I am of a sensible nature rather than a romantic one, so that I am inclined to look at problems from a practical point of view.'

He smiled indulgently.

'If that is your nature, then I love it, but, no, I mustn't say so. You must realise that not only is Fox Wood saved but the Ellerton cottages, too. What do you think of that?'

She laughed with delight.

'I am so pleased, Mr . . . Aubrey, I should say. I am so pleased and happy I could kiss you.'

'I don't mind, Laura,' he said pulling her into his arms, and they kissed again. 'And now we must do the real talking. Will you marry me, Laura?'

She stared at him wondering if she had heard correctly.

'Marry you?' she stammered. 'But you cannot even ask me, Aubrey. I am one of the servants. Do not speak so foolishly.'

'Let me ask you something else then. Do you love me?'

Laura felt herself go pink for she had found out that she loved Mr Aubrey Greene very much indeed. But to be his wife? How could she? But she replied truthfully.

'Aubrey, I know now that I love you but that is an end to it. The nurserymaid cannot become the wife of the son of the house, you must know that.'

'Laura, my dearest girl, you know as well as I do that you are a young lady from a very old Yorkshire family. You are as well-born as I am. I know that your father left you in difficult circumstances and that you had to seek employment, but you were not exactly a typical nurserymaid, you must admit. So I will ask you again. I love you very much, please, will you marry me, Laura?'

Laura stood very still. The words were going to be too difficult.

'Thank you very much, Aubrey, for asking, but my reply still has to be no.'

He looked bewildered.

'But why, Laura, why? We love each other, I can offer you a splendid home for Roxby Hall is big enough for three families.'

Laura intcrrupted quickly.

'That is just the trouble, Aubrey. Your father would never receive me as your wife after my behaviour. Surely you can see that.'

'No, Laura, my father did what was correct. He dismissed a servant who had spoken out of turn. But when I re-introduce you as Miss Laura Fawcett of Petrie Lodge and tell him what was achieved at Fox Wood, I believe that he, and my mother, will welcome you with open arms as a daughter. Will you let me take you to them now? We will call at Petrie Lodge to say where we are going. Please, Laura,' he whispered and bent and kissed her lips to try and coax her.

Laura's senses stirred her into submission.

'Very well,' she whispered in return and they hurried back to the gig and were soon on their way to Roxby Hall.

They met Janice in the garden with the children and they all ran up to the gig, with laughter and excitement.

Aubrey called to his sister.

'I have asked Laura to marry me, Janice, and she has refused me.'

'Refused?' Janice cried. 'But she loves you. I have guessed it for a long time.'

Laura butted in.

'Janice, your father will not approve,' she said quietly.

'Come along, Laura, let us go and see him,' Aubrey urged and he and Laura hurried into the Hall.

Lady Dorothy was on her own in the drawing-room and looked unhappy.

'Aubrey, Laura, what is it? Your father is very upset, Aubrey. He feels he was too strict with Laura and you went off without telling him the whole story of what had happened at Fox Wood after he had left the scene, though I do understand that it is saved. Ah, here he is. He must have heard you arrive.'

She turned to her husband.

'Aubrey and Laura are here, Henry.'

'So I see. What is it all about?'

Aubrey went up and shook his father by the

hand.

'Father, first of all, I want to tell you that after Laura's suggestion to Mr Fortescue at Fox Wood yesterday, the whole matter was settled amicably and the railway line will take the lower route by the river thus avoiding the Ellerton cottages and Fox Wood, and also Sir Rowland's property. Father, are you all right?'

Sir Henry sat down heavily next to his wife.

'I have been too hard on Laura. Oh, she is here.'

Aubrey continued as though there had been no interruption.

'I have asked Laura to be my wife and she has refused me because she thinks you will not approve.'

Sir Henry jumped up, a different person.

'Refused? Goodness gracious, can't have that.'

He took Laura by the hand.

'Must apologise for dismissing you so quickly. Thought better of it after you had gone. You spoke bravely and very sensibly and it has all been resolved. Do you wish to marry Aubrey, then? We would welcome you as a daughter, wouldn't we, Dorothy?'

They all laughed and Janice came in to see what the noise was about. Wine was produced and there were congratulations and happiness all round.

In the middle of it all, Aubrey and Laura crept into the garden. He took her in his arms and kissed her gently.

'Now I can ask you again. Will you marry me, Miss Laura?'

'Yes, please, Mr Aubrey,' was the happy reply.

We hope you have enjoyed this Large Print book. Other Chivers Press or Thorndike Press Large Print books are available at your library or directly from the publishers.

For more information about current and forthcoming titles, please call or write, without obligation, to:

Chivers Large Print
published by BBC Audiobooks Ltd
St James House, The Square
Lower Bristol Road
Bath BA2 3SB
UK
email: bbcaudiobooks@bbc.co.uk
www.bbcaudiobooks.co.uk

OR

Thorndike Press
295 Kennedy Memorial Drive
Waterville
Maine 04901
USA
www.gale.com/thorndike
www.gale.com/wheeler

All our Large Print titles are designed for easy reading, and all our books are made to last.